# THREE'S A COVEN

## WESTERN WOODS MYSTERY #3

SAMANTHA SILVER

BLUEBERRY BOOKS PRESS

## CHAPTER 1

"*Is* that supposed to be on fire?"

I looked at the cauldron my friend and roommate Ellie was working on, which currently had glittery purple and red flames shooting from it towards the ceiling.

"Of course," Ellie grinned. "How else am I supposed to make brown butter brownies?"

"By browning the butter in a pot on the stove, like a normal person?"

"There's no fun in that. Besides, the flames weren't to brown the butter. They were to create the fiery desire that a person feels when they eat the brownies."

"So basically, you're making love potion brownies?" I asked, poking my head into the now-extinguished cauldron. It just looked like normal brownie mixture to me, with bits of red and purple glitter mixed into the batter.

"Well, it's not necessary *love* that the eater feels. Whatever the eater needs most in the world, they feel the desire to get it done. So it's great for when you're doing something super boring at work but you know you need to get it done, or when you've been putting off doing the laundry for the last week because life just keeps getting in the way."

"Ah," I nodded. "Nice. Is that for the coffee shop?"

"Nah, I only make food to serve customers when I'm at work. I'm sure you can guess which workaholic this batch is for."

"Amy?" I asked with a small grin, and Ellie smiled.

"Sure is. She begged me to make them for her since she didn't have the time to make a batch herself. She has an important exam coming up that she's convinced she isn't studying enough for."

"Right. Because that sounds exactly like her."

"That's what I said. But of course, with Amy, getting ninety percent is basically a failing grade."

"It *is* a failing grade," Amy said, rushing down the stairs. Her dark eyes darted all over the place, and her pixie-cut hair was somehow disheveled. "What's even the point of living if you've only gotten eighty-seven percent in Advanced Planetary Mathematical Structure and Movement?"

Ellie hid a smile and raised her eyebrows at me as if to say "see?"

"You know, I think maybe you're taking this exam a little bit too seriously," I said.

"*Too seriously?*" Amy said, turning on me, and I involuntarily took a step back. Wow. Amy could be *scary* when she wanted to be.

"Never mind, you're obviously in complete control of your emotions right now," I replied.

"How long until you're going to be finished?" Amy asked, looking at Ellie.

"About thirty minutes. The ingredients just need to cook in the oven."

"So even magical baking has to happen in an oven? You can't just use a spell to do it?" I asked, peering into the cauldron as Ellie got a baking dish out from underneath the stove.

"Nope," Ellie replied. "What happens to molecules from baking is actually so complex that we eventually found it easier to just use an oven to do it rather than to try and figure out a way to speed up the process with magic. However, that doesn't mean we can't add magic to the cooking."

"Cool," I replied as Ellie slipped the baking tray into the oven.

"Hey, we might be witches, but we're still inherently lazy. Why come up with a convoluted magical way of doing something when the human way works better? I think some of the fire covens have discovered ways of improving cooking methods with magic – one day I'm hoping to be invited to one of their covens to learn some of their ways – but we just use plain old ovens."

"Right. How long will those brownies take to cook?" Amy asked.

"Twenty-two minutes," Ellie replied.

"I'll be back then. I haven't got even a minute to waste," Amy replied, turning on her heel and heading right back to her room.

Ellie laughed. "See? Amy on exam day is definitely a bundle of nerves."

"No kidding. Have you guys not heard of Xanax?"

"She thrives on the anxiety. Says it makes her work better. She refuses any sort of magical or human aid."

"That sounds about right." It did sound like exactly the sort of thing Amy would say.

I hung out with Ellie while we waited for the brownies to cook. A part of me didn't really want to eat the magical part – after all, I had absolutely planned on having a lazy day today – but at the same time, a part of me was curious, too.

When they came out of the oven, Amy walked into the room at the exact moment that Ellie opened the oven door.

"Wow, that was some good timing," I said, impressed.

"I managed to go over my definition of an ellipse by the directrix property notes," Amy said. "Now, I really need those brownies. The exam starts in six hours."

"Alright, alright," Ellie said, handing her over four brownies on a plate, steam still rising from the chocolatey goodness. Amy took the plate, thanked Ellie and quickly disappeared once more.

"I assume she's always been like this?" I asked, reaching for a brownie myself.

"Let me put it this way: when we were in the second year at the academy, so still little kids, Amy misread a question and got ninety percent on a test instead of one hundred. She cried for the entire afternoon, then swore she would never get such a low mark again. She studied so hard for the next test the teacher actually ended up giving her *over* a hundred percent because she was that far in front of the rest of us. And she really was. I mean, I was still basically eating crayons, compared to her."

I laughed. "I actually believe that story one hundred percent."

"It's completely accurate. She's been like this her entire life. She actually thrives on this kind of pressure."

"Well, I think it would drive me insane," I said, taking a bite of the brownie. The soft texture, somewhere between fudge-like and cake-like melted in my mouth, with an added taste of browned caramel floating through. I closed my eyes and savored the bite, letting the sweet sugar sit on my tongue.

"This is so good," I said as I swallowed. "You're amazing, Ellie."

"Thanks," Ellie grinned. "Now enjoy spending your

afternoon doing something you really, really needed to get done."

About thirty seconds later, my brain zoned in on something I'd been putting off for a bit: really making my room my own. I headed back towards it with a determination that I was going to really, truly settle in here.

"Wow, someone's on a mission," my cat familiar, Mr. Meowgi, said from the spot on the comforter he was currently occupying.

"I'm going to do this," I said, reaching into the bag I'd brought a few things from the human world in and organizing the books on a small shelf. To be honest, there wasn't that much to do, but an hour later my room was a lot more organized, and a little bit more *me*. I made a note to buy some things in town for my room; a few nice pieces of art on the walls could be a good way to really bring the room together.

It was funny; this was the first time since my mom had died that I really felt *home*. When I lived alone in Seattle I always made a point of not decorating. Decorating would get me too attached to a place, which I couldn't afford when I was working minimum-wage jobs and finding myself moving from place to place fairly regularly.

When I was finished, I put my hands on my hips and admired my handiwork. My books were now on the shelf, I had moved the bed around – much to Mr. Meowgi's disgust – so that the afternoon sun fell on the bed, and I had taken a few of the succulents from the garden outside and moved them onto my dresser. I had called up Ellie to help with a spell, and she had turned the pots from simple terra-cotta to beautiful glittering pink, blue, and orange that shimmered in the light.

Yes, this was definitely much better.

"Hey Ellie, do you want to come into town and find some art with me?" I asked as I made my way into the kitchen. Just then I noticed Sara sitting at the counter staring at the brownies.

"Sure," Ellie replied. "I'm just fixing up another batch of brownies for Sara without the focus spell added in."

"I've been at work all day; the last thing I want to do is actually focus on anything, but those brownies smelled so good I begged Ellie to make more," she said.

"Oh good, you've saved me from doing the same thing," I giggled. "Want to come along? Thanks to that first batch I spent the afternoon redecorating, and now that I've been working on it I kind of want to get it finished completely."

"Thanks, but I think I'm going to just veg out for the rest of the night," Sara said, poking a finger in the cauldron Ellie was carefully adding ingredients into, chanting incantations at the various ingredients and making them rise up and fall straight into the large, cast-iron pot.

"TV and brownies does sound good."

"You guys had better leave soon before all the stores close."

"True. If I put these in the oven, can I trust you to take them out in twenty-two minutes?" Ellie asked.

"Of course," Sara replied. "I mean, of course normally the answer would be no, but seeing as there are delicious brownies on the line, I will watch the clock like my life depends on it."

I laughed as I ran back to my room to grab my purse as Ellie and I headed out into the night.

## CHAPTER 2

"How long do magical exams take?" I asked Ellie as we headed out. Summer was coming to an end; it was late August now and the first signs of the crisp fall were in the air. It still wasn't jacket weather – we did live in the Pacific Northwest, after all – but that time of year was definitely on its way. I briefly wondered where exactly Western Woods *was*. After all, I knew we were still generally in the Seattle area, but that was all I knew. Where *did* magical towns build themselves? It wasn't like you could type the name into Google Maps.

As Ellie began to answer, though, I decided that was a question for another time.

"It depends on the class. In the basic classes, the ones Sara and I did, which are the ones almost all witches end with, they generally take about one to two hours. We don't actually do exams until the later years, until we turn fifteen. Some of them are way shorter. For example, when we took *Introduction to Jupiter's Spells,* the exam only took about twenty minutes per person. We had to see the professor individually and perform about ten different spells that we'd learned that year, so it didn't really take all that long. But *A History of Covens* was a two-hour sit-down exam comprised of two hundred multiple choice questions."

"Ugh," I shuddered. "That reminds me of calculus."

"What's calculus?" Ellie asked.

"Like math, only harder."

"Ew."

After a few minutes, Ellie led me into a cute little cottage near the outskirts of town. It was part of a row of four cottages, all painted a different pastel color, but all keeping with the same European-style shutters and design. This one was a robin's egg blue, with a sign above the door reading "Once Upon a Trinket".

"Is this going to be the kind of shop with kitschy things like the ones my grandmother loved?" I asked with a bit of a frown. That definitely was not my style.

"Oh, just you wait," Ellie replied with a grin. "It's absolutely not like that at all."

I followed after her as Ellie made her way through the front door, the bell above tinkling to indicate our entrance. I stood in the entrance, stunned as I looked around.

This was basically as if someone had taken all the

best things you could get in an Etsy store and made them real. And made them *magical*.

To my left was a set of metal shelves, with rectangular wicker baskets set on an angle to better display the products they were offering. It was obviously filled with bath bombs, and as I read the descriptions on some of them, I knew this wasn't exactly the sort of thing I would buy at Lush.

*The Gift of Gab: Making an important presentation? Going to a party and you're not the chatty type? This bath bomb will make the user feel confident and outgoing for the six hours following its use.*

*Fairy Fairy Happy: Feeling down? This bath bomb releases a scent that will give you temporarily relief from whatever is bringing you pain at the moment. Please limit use to one per day, and use for no longer than one week at a time. See a Healer if you feel your depression to be serious.*

*Big Blue Baby: Looking to bring a new baby witch, wizard, fairy, or vampire into this world? Take a bath with this bomb six hours before your next mating ritual to improve your chances of success.*

Wow. Those were certainly some serious claims.

"Do these actually work?" I whispered to Ellie, motioning to the bath bombs, and she nodded.

"Of course. Ceres, the fairy who owns this store, has a witch who works for her and makes a bunch of the magical stuff, like the potions that go into the bath bombs.

"Wow," I said, making a mental note to look at the

rest of the bath bombs later. After all, there was just so much *stuff* everywhere. There were cute purses that promised only the owner could reach inside to get anything. Pillowcases with cute slogans like "Not a basic witch", "If you've got it, haunt it", and "I'm fairy adorable" were surrounded by handmade leather collars for familiars, which a sign promised could be personalized. Special "vampire approved" sunscreen sat on a shelf next to glitter saver – apparently, for the fairy who thought her wings needed a little bit more shimmer than what was natural.

I was so caught up in looking at all the little knick-knacks in the store that I didn't even notice when a fairy, taller than the other ones I'd met at almost four feet, came fluttering over towards us. Her long, blonde hair was tied back in a ponytail that reached her lower back, and her pale purple wings fluttered effortlessly behind her as she looked at us from behind large blue eyes.

"Hello there, witches. Can I help you find anything today?"

"No, thanks, Ceres," Ellie replied. "Tina is looking for some decorations for her room, and I'm pretty sure she's overwhelmed just by the sheer number of things in here, so I think we'll just look around for a while.

"Ah, you're the new witch in town," Ceres said with a nod. "Sorry, we usually get a decent number of tourists in here, so I'm never sure who's a permanent fixture and who isn't."

"Yeah, that's me," I said with a shy smile. "I'm Tina."

"Ceres. It's nice to meet you. I hope you're feeling welcome in town."

"Absolutely, everyone's been incredibly kind to me."

"That's wonderful to hear. Well, please let me know if you need any help, I'll be behind the counter."

"Thanks so much," I said as Ceres floated away back towards the front of the store.

"Come here, check out these wall hangings," Ellie suggested, taking me towards the wall at the far right of the store. "How about something like this?" She motioned to a large print on the wall with a motivational message: "Life is tough, my darling, but so are you." Not too bad. I gasped, however, as suddenly the letters began moving, shifting themselves around into a different message. "If not now, then when?"

"How about things that don't move?" I suggested. "There's enough magic all around me right now, I think I want my room to be one little reminder that I used to live life without it. How about something like this?" I made my way over to another print, made of four planks of wood, with a calming picture of the ocean printed onto it. I figured it was fitting, seeing as I was from a water coven, apparently. "This isn't going to change into anything, is it?"

Ellie shook her head. "Doesn't look like it. We can ask Ceres to be sure. That's really cute, you should definitely get it."

I picked up the wooden art off the wall and began

to take it to the counter. On my way there, I also passed a small rusted cactus sculpture that I figured would look good on the dresser with my succulents on it, so I grabbed that as well.

"Perfect, is that everything for you?" Ceres asked as I made my way to the counter.

"Yeah, I think so. This art piece, it doesn't do anything magical, does it?" I asked, motioning to my wooden ocean painting.

"No, not at all," Ceres said with a smile. "I like to keep a mix of magical and non-magical items in here. Some of my customers find things from the human world to be incredibly fun novelties."

I smiled to myself at the idea of something that didn't move on its own being a novelty as Ceres packed things up for me, and Ellie paid her.

"Thanks," I said to her warmly. "I'm really going to have to get a job here soon."

"Don't worry about it," Ellie said, waving a hand away. "The coven can easily afford it. You need to take the time to actually become a witch."

I nodded as I watched Ceres put the items in the magical delivery box, which I knew was going to send the items directly into our living room back home.

"All right! Your items are delivered. Have a great night," Ceres told us with a smile, and just as Ellie and I left the store, the magical "open" sign at the front of the store that shimmered from an invisible source changed to a red "closed" instead.

"I guess Amy's test is starting," I said, looking at my phone to check the time. Sure enough, it was five-oh-one. "How long do you have to wait for your test results in the magical world?"

"What do you mean?" Ellie replied, tilting her head.

"How long does it take the teachers to mark all your exams? A few days?"

Ellie laughed. "Oh, no. It's instant."

"Magic?" I asked, and Ellie nodded.

"Yes. For the classes that involve practical work during exams the professor gives you your mark right then and there, and for written exams, the professor creates a special potion that basically marks the work instantly. You hand the professor your exam, they dip it in the potion, and it comes up completely marked."

"Wow, that would certainly save a lot of stress compared to my high school experience," I muttered.

"Hold on one second," Ellie said as her phone rang. She pulled it out of her purse and frowned as she looked at the caller. "Why would Amy be calling me in the middle of an exam?"

She swiped at the screen to answer the call, but before she even had a chance to say hello, I could hear Amy's voice, more panicked than I'd ever heard, screeching through the phone.

"Ellie, you have to come over here. *Now*. Oh my God, I can't believe this."

"Amy, calm down. What's happened?" Ellie asked, raising her eyebrows at me. I could hear the conversation almost perfectly, despite the phone not being on speaker; that was how loudly Amy was yelling. There was no way Amy would have been late to her exam and not allowed in. Amy was the type of person who would have been sitting next to the door to be let in an hour before the exam, no question about it.

"It's Professor Lei. She's dead!"

## CHAPTER 3

"Whoa, whoa, hold on a second. What do you mean, dead?" Ellie asked.

"Just get over here. I need you!"

"All right," Ellie said. "Tina and I will be there in five minutes."

"Hurry."

Ellie hung up the phone and looked at me. "Did you hear that?"

I nodded. "Let's go."

Five minutes later, we were at the coven headquarters, a whitewashed brick building with a green dome on top. This time, however, I didn't stop to admire the grandeur of the building; instead I followed Ellie inside straight away.

I had only been down the hall to see the head of the coven before, but this time as we entered, Ellie led me to the right and up a flight of dark mahogany stairs with elaborately carved railings to an elevated walk-way. About ten feet down, she turned and led me through a door, which led to another hall, but this time there were about a half dozen faces, all of which looked like they belonged to terrified witches and wizards.

As soon as we came in, Amy rushed towards us. "Oh, you guys, it's awful!"

"Calm down, Amy. Come over here, tell us what happened."

"Well, the eight of us, we were all waiting out here for the exam to start. Professor Lei has always been extremely punctual; she doesn't open the door until two minutes before the start of the exam. So when that time passed, we all began to wonder what was going on. Oh Jupiter, I can't believe it."

"Relax, take a couple deep breaths," I said. "What happened next?"

"Well, when five o'clock passed, and we still hadn't seen any sign of her, we began to wonder what was going on. So I used a spell to get into the locked room, and that was where we found her. She was on the floor."

"Has anyone told Chief Enforcer King?" I asked, and Amy nodded mutely.

"Yes. As soon as we found the body, one of the wizards went to check for a pulse, but there was none. Someone else ran off to get Chief Enforcer King. That was when I called you. I didn't know what else to do."

"You need to go downstairs, find Lita, and tell her what happened," Ellie said. "Do you understand?"

Amy's eyes widened. "Oh my goodness. I didn't even think. Of course someone needs to tell Lita."

"Bring her up here, ok?" Ellie said. Amy nodded.

"I will. I will. Ok, I'll be back."

Amy rushed down the stairs, and Ellie shook her head sadly. "Professor Lei was nice. I had her for an astronomy class once, in my last year at the Academy."

Less than a minute later, Amy came rushing back up the stairs with Lita, the leader of the coven, following only steps behind her. For a witch of her size, Lita was surprisingly agile, and as soon as she entered the room everything fell silent as every witch and wizard turned their eyes to their leader.

Despite her small stature, Lita was a very imposing force. "Thank you everyone, for staying here," she announced. "I will ask you to stay for just a little bit longer, until Jennifer returns with Chief Enforcer King, as she may want to speak with all of you."

"She's in here," Amy whispered, motioning to a thick, windowless door. Lita gave a curt nod, and stepped inside. I couldn't help myself; I followed after her, Ellie hot on my heels.

My eyes immediately focused on the witch at the front of the room. There were two long, wide tables with benches on either side of them, papers for all the witches and wizards getting ready to take their exams sitting on top of them. The witch was in the middle of the room, between the two tables. It looked like she had simply fallen forward; there was no blood or anything on the floor. I was half tempted to make sure she hadn't passed out. Her long, black hair splayed around her like a deathly halo, and Lita immediately made her way towards the body and checked for a pulse herself.

"Oh, Mai. Rest in peace, my dear friend," I heard Lita mumble quietly before she stood up and looked at Ellie and me.

"I am going to ask the two of you to leave," she said. "Until a cause of death has been determined, this room is officially off-limits."

Ellie and I nodded. I suddenly felt a little bit embarrassed; here Lita was mourning the loss of a friend, and Ellie and I had gone in to watch simply from morbid curiosity. The two of us shuffled out of the room, and Ellie pulled me out into the main hall.

"I think Professor Lei was murdered," she said to me in a hushed tone.

"What? That's ridiculous," I replied. "What on earth makes you think that?"

"Well, the way Lita immediately kicked us out of the room."

"She was probably just being careful. Maybe it was a heart attack, or something. It's not like there were any signs that she was hit over the head or anything."

"It could have been, but Professor Lei was a healthy, relatively young witch. She was in her early forties, I think. Besides, Lita must have seen something that made her think this might not have been natural, or she wouldn't have kicked us out of the room."

"Or maybe she just didn't want us gawking over the body of her dead friend."

"I guess," Ellie admitted. "Still, you have to admit it's weird, dying so suddenly like that."

"Not that weird," I said quietly. One morning not that long ago, I'd woken up expecting it to be just another day. By the end of it I had become an orphan.

Before Ellie got a chance to reply, a wizard who looked to be around thirty-five, with dark brown hair plastered to his head, came rushing into the room, completely out of breath.

"Oliver?" Amy asked. "Where's Chief Enforcer King?"

"I can't find her," the man replied, panting. "I've been all over town. She's nowhere to be found."

Ellie and I exchanged a look. This was getting weirder by the minute.

# CHAPTER 4

"What do you mean, she can't be found?"

"Exactly what it sounds like. I went to her office, and was told by the wolf shifter that she went out a little while ago. He didn't know where, so he used this stone the shifters use to see where she is, but apparently her location didn't show up at all. So he went with me into her office. Sure enough, nothing there. Then we went everywhere we could think of that she might be, and nothing. No one in town has seen her in the last three hours."

Amy frowned. "There's got to be a mistake, somewhere. Chief Enforcer King wouldn't just leave without telling anyone. She's got to be somewhere, you must have just missed her."

Oliver shook his head vehemently. "No. No, we

didn't. We looked all over, and the wolf said he should have been able to smell her scent around, and he couldn't. I don't know where Chief Enforcer King is, but she's not here."

"Well, she may have gone to a neighboring town for an investigation, or something," Amy offered.

"Exactly," Lita's voice said. "I'm sure Chief Enforcer King is completely fine. Now, if she's unavailable at the moment I don't see the point in the rest of you staying here indefinitely. Please, go back to your homes, and please refrain from speculating on what's happened here. I'm sure Professor Lei has just passed away from an unfortunate health issue. It's a tragedy, but for the sake of her family, please don't go spreading around unfounded rumors. Now, if you'll excuse me, I need to go tell her husband and daughter what has happened."

The room was silent as Lita left, and I couldn't help but notice as she walked past that her eyes were just a little bit on the glassy side. She was definitely not about to have an easy conversation.

After she left, the door closing with a soft sound behind her, the low hum of conversation rose up in the room once more. Amy made her way towards Ellie and me.

"I can't believe this," Amy said, shaking her head.

"I want to know where Chief Enforcer King is," Ellie replied.

"It is a little bit strange, isn't it, that she can't be

found. If she'd gone to a nearby town, wouldn't she have told one of the other Enforcers first?" Amy asked.

I nodded. "Chief Enforcer King doesn't seem to me to be the type to do that."

"So what, do you guys think there might be something wrong?"

I shrugged. "I don't know. I mean, maybe? It might be nothing. Maybe she's just got a lot on her plate, and she decided to slip out for a minute. But I think it could be possible it's more than that."

"In that case, I think it might be linked to what happened with Professor Lei," Amy suggested.

"Really? Why do you think that?" Ellie asked.

"Well, it's just that this morning I was out running and doing equations – I always find that if I stress my body and force it to recall facts while I'm stressed is a great way to see if I'm adequately prepared, since test conditions often aren't ideal – and I saw Professor Lei walking into the Town Hall. I can't say for sure she was going to see Chief Enforcer King, but she does work out of there."

I frowned. "So what do you think? Maybe Professor Lei saw something she shouldn't have, and that person came after her and Chief Enforcer King?"

"I don't know," Amy shrugged. "What I do know is that I saw the two of them together this morning, so it's possible that the death of one and disappearance of the other aren't completely isolated incidents."

"If they are linked, we also need to be prepared to have Chief Enforcer King's body show up at some point, too," Ellie said quietly, and I shuddered. I didn't know Professor Lei at all, but I'd had a few conversations with Chief Enforcer King. I liked her. I thought she was a good head of law enforcement in town, and I really, really hoped that wherever she was, she was fine.

"So what happens now? I mean, with Professor Lei and everything?"

"I guess Lita will take care of everything," Amy shrugged. "She's the head of the coven after all. Chief Enforcer King does have other enforcers around; I'm sure one of them will take over the investigation."

"We need to get into that room," Ellie said. "After all, isn't there a spell that you can use to determine what a cause of death was?"

Amy crossed her arms. "Absolutely not. I'm not doing that. I liked Professor Lei, and I don't want to ruin any dignity she might have left. Besides, Lita told us she's going to take care of it, so let's leave it with her."

"Fine," Ellie replied. "Let's head home then. But I don't like this. I don't like this one bit."

I was definitely with Ellie on this one. It might've been due to the paranormal world, but I knew one thing: Chief Enforcer King was reliable, and a great cop. If she was missing, then something was very wrong.

≈

*T*he three of us headed home, and I quickly put my new purchases up in my room. However, this time, my mind was on other things. Where was Chief Enforcer King? Had Professor Lei died of natural causes? If not, was the death and the disappearance linked? I had a ton of questions, and virtually no answers.

When I made my way down to the living room once more, I found the other two girls catching Sara up on what had happened.

"That's absolutely awful," Sara said. "Let me find out from my mom which Healer they're going to send to look at the body."

"Is that how it works?" I asked. "Do they just send a Healer? You don't have a medical examiner who specifically deals with dead bodies to establish cause of death?"

Amy smiled. "No, there is no real need for that here. The Healers learn special spells, at least, the witch Healers do, which allows them to determine cause of death much more easily than a human examination would."

"What about things in a murder that a medical examiner would normally look at?" I asked. "Things like stomach contents, or any old injuries that might be relevant to a murder investigation."

"Well, the thing is, there usually aren't all that many murderers here in Western Woods. The last couple have certainly been the exception rather than the rule," Ellie explained. "So, most of the time there is no real need for that sort of investigation. But, if there is, I believe that all of the Healers are trained in the examination of dead bodies as well as live ones."

"That's right," Sara confirmed. "My mom always tells me how her least favorite topic when she was learning to be a Healer was the examination of dead bodies. She can do it, but she really hates it. She feels like it's such an invasion of privacy, and that the dead deserve more dignity than that."

"I think the bigger indignity would be letting a person's murderer go free because the Enforcers didn't have enough evidence to solve the crime," Amy said. "Anyway, I'm sure this is all just a misunderstanding and Chief Enforcer King will come back sooner rather than later. She might just be visiting with another coven or something. Now, since my exam has been put off indefinitely, would you like to do an extra lesson with me, Tina?"

"Sure," I nodded. As much as Amy could be neurotic and a huge know it all, I very much enjoyed my lessons with her, and now that I had lived in Western Woods for about a month, I was finally starting to feel like a real witch from time to time, thanks to the spells she had been teaching me.

"Good," Amy said. "Why don't you go and grab your journal? I've realized that we haven't done any lessons about the different planets, their elements, and how they link together. There's a lot of magical history that you need to learn about as well as the practical aspect of doing spells."

I nodded, running to my room and grabbing one of the journals I'd bought that was still blank, bringing it back to the living room with a pen. To be honest, I was actually looking forward to this sort of lesson. The more I learned about how magic was connected to celestial beings and their various elements, the more interested I became in that sort of thing. Plus, a part of me was really excited to potentially learn more about where my parents came from. After all, I knew absolutely nothing about them, and that included what coven they were from. We were fairly certain that I was a descendent of a water-based coven, but beyond that we didn't know.

When I got back, Ellie was busy reading my copy of *Harry Potter and the Sorcerer's Stone*, with her face completely buried in the book. Sara sat on the other couch with her legs brought up to her knees, and she smiled at me when I came back into the room.

"Do you mind if I listen in on Amy's lesson?" Sara asked. "After all, I could use a refresher course on a lot of this stuff."

"Of course," I said. "If you want, you can borrow my notes that I take as well."

"Thank you so much," Sara beamed. "You never know, maybe really getting this stuff engrained will help me with my spells."

"It absolutely should," Amy explained. "Especially when performing spells that originate with other covens. I know you rarely do it, but sometimes it is a necessity."

"I'll settle with being able to perform Jupiter's spells without messing anything up too badly, first," Sara replied. Her magic definitely had a unique quality to it – in that whenever she tried a spell, it was a mystery what was going to happen, but it usually wasn't what the spell was meant to do.

"Your confidence level will increase the more theoretical knowledge you have," Amy said. "So yes, absolutely sit in on this. Now, I want to start with a basic lesson in which covens are governed by which elements. There are hundreds of covens out there, each governed by a different element, but there are about twenty important ones which all witches need to know. Which ones do you know already?"

"Well, obviously the coven of Jupiter is thunder," I said. "And, um, Mercury is water, and Io is fire. Those are the only three I remember."

Amy turned to Sara. "What can you add to that?"

"Ok, let me think. The other thunder covens are Venus, Dione, and Hyperion. I think there's another one too, but I can't think of it. The water ones I know are Mercury, Neptune, the moon, and... Europa. Earth is Phobos, Deimos, and Callipso, and Fire I only know Io and Mars."

I jotted down the celestial beings Sara rattled off as quickly as I could, trying to keep up.

"Good," Amy nodded. "The other coven of thunder that you missed is Miranda."

"Right," Sara said. "I never remember the ones that were named after those people that human wrote about."

"You mean William Shakespeare," Amy said.

"That's the one. What a strange name."

"Hey, just be glad you didn't have to study the works he actually *wrote*," I said.

"Why, are they bad?"

"No, I wouldn't say they're *bad*. They're just written in super old English from like five hundred years ago, and so they're kind of hard to follow, especially when you're like, fourteen."

Sara wrinkled her nose while Amy glared at the two of us. "Right. Well, if you're done talking about that, do you have all of the thunder covens written down?"

She looked at me, and I nodded. "Jupiter, Venus, Dione, Hyperion, and Miranda."

"Good. Now, the water covens are the most important, because you're one of them. We just don't know which, yet. The main water covens are, as Sara said, Mercury, Neptune, the moon, and Europa. There's also Pluto, Ganymede, Cerys, and Titan."

I wrote down the names in my journal and looked back up at Amy.

"Now, the main fire covens are Mars, Io, Charon, Enceladus, and Mimas. Then, for the air covens, you have Saturn, Uranus, Oberon, Ariel, and Titania."

"There's some more Shakespearean characters for you," I said to Sara with a grin. "You should read *As You Like It*, it might help you remember them."

"*A Midsummer Night's Dream* might be even more useful, seeing as that's the play that features the characters those moons are named after," Amy replied, giving me a 'you should have known better' look.

"Oh, whoops. How do you even know that? You didn't sneak over to the human world and take some high school English courses, did you?"

"No, but seeing as the people in the human world are our neighbors I found it important to learn what's important to them and their culture as well," Amy said.

"That's maybe the most Amy thing I've ever heard," Sara snickered.

"I'm choosing to take that as a compliment."

"To be honest, it was one. As much as I make fun of you, I wish I had your ability to learn things."

"You would, if you just applied yourself and stopped changing the subject constantly like this. We still have to go through the earth covens. Those are Phobos, Deimos, Callisto, Rhea, Iapetus, Umbriel, and Tethys."

"Ok," I said as I wrote them down in my notebook as well. "Got it."

"Good. Now, you'll need to memorize those. Let's go over the importance of covens when it comes to spells, and how an element affects a witch's magic."

I got my pen at the ready; I was eager and ready to learn.

## CHAPTER 5

The next morning, when I woke up, Ellie and Amy were both sitting in the kitchen, eating some oatmeal for breakfast. I grabbed a bowl full from the cauldron that Ellie had obviously made, along with a banana and a handful of blueberries, and joined them at the dining table.

"Any news from Chief Enforcer King?" I asked.

Amy shook her head. "No. I was working with Lita last night. When I left an hour ago she still hadn't shown up at all. No one knows where she is, and people are starting to worry."

"No kidding," I muttered.

"Someone needs to do something," Ellie said. "There's been a death, *and* our Chief Enforcer is missing. At the very least, someone needs to try and find out why."

"As long as that someone isn't us," Amy said, giving Ellie a pointed look.

"Why not? After all, Professor Lei was part of our coven. And I don't know about you, but I'd rather get Chief Enforcer King back sooner rather than later."

"That's what the other Enforcers are for."

"And if something has happened to Chief Enforcer King, that's what the person who did something to her will be expecting. They won't be expecting us to look for her, though."

"That doesn't mean we should be the ones to do anything," Amy argued. "We have absolutely no training in law enforcement."

"But we have the smartest witch in the coven on our side. Who else is going to be able to figure out what happened?"

"The shifter Enforcers who have multiple years of training in solving cases."

"We have experience, though. We – and by that I mainly mean Tina – has already solved two murders since arriving in Western Woods."

A small blush crept up my face. "It was a team effort, though," I said. Especially when it came to saving my life afterwards.

Amy threw up her hands. "Absolutely not. Let the Enforcers try and find King. If it turns out Professor Lei has been murdered, then ok, we can help look into it. But only because Chief Enforcer King isn't around to help right now."

Ellie winked at me. "It's only a matter of time before she caves completely."

~

*L*ater that day, Sara had promised me we could go down to the hospital and talk to her mom. I needed some career advice. It wasn't that I wanted to become a Healer; I didn't. Well, not a Healer for regular paranormals, anyway. I wanted to become the equivalent of a magical vet, which was a job that didn't exist yet. The problem was, not only was I a witch who didn't know how to be a witch yet – sure, I could do some basic spells, but I was nowhere near the same skill level as the others in the coven – but I was really pushing a boulder uphill by deciding that I wanted to do something that didn't even exist as a job in the magical world.

Luckily, Sara's mom was one of the town's most renowned Healers, and she was willing to meet with me to help determine how I could go about becoming an Animal Healer.

The two of us walked to Hexpresso Bean, where we had planned on meeting Heather Neach. I had to admit, I was a bit nervous.

"Relax," Sara said, making me realize my nerves weren't being kept quite as under wraps as I'd hoped. "It's going to be fine."

"Thanks," I said with a smile. "I feel silly just considering this as a career path. I mean, I don't even know how to be a normal witch yet. Who am I to think that I can start a whole new career here that no one else has even considered before?"

"Hey, don't think that way. You're not nearly as bad of a witch as you think. I mean, I don't have anything to compare it to since we don't have any other witches here who started as adults, but you're learning incredibly quickly. You're already a better witch than I am, and you have just the right kind of attitude to be able to make a real big change like this."

"I'm not a better witch than you," I said as we snagged a couple of seats and a table by the far wall.

"Oh, you are. Don't worry, I'm not offended or anything. But it's a fact. When you cast a spell, the spell does what it's supposed to do."

"Yeah, but you know hundreds, probably thousands of spells. I can count the number of spells I know on both hands."

"That will come with time. But, when you cast a spell, it always does what it's supposed to. And to be honest, I'm surprised at how powerfully you manage considering Jupiter isn't your coven. There's something really natural to your magic."

"Thanks," I said, a small blush coming to my cheeks. "I appreciate you saying that."

"Now, what do you want to eat?"

"Surprise me," I smiled as Sara made her way to the

counter to order from the fluttering fairy I recognized as Aurora.

A minute later, while I was letting my mind wander, a woman who looked like an older version of Sara, with the same fiery red hair, freckles and green eyes sat down at one of the other chairs.

"Hello, Tina. How are you doing?"

"Heather, hi," I said with a smile. "Thanks so much for meeting me."

"Of course. It's always a pleasure to help guide a young witch."

Sara made her way back over and squeezed her mom's hand quickly. "Hi, mom."

"Hello, dear. I see you've got a day off from your job."

Sara nodded. "I have, yes."

Sara and her jobs were always a bit of a touchy subject with her mother. Heather had grown up expecting Sara to follow in her shoes and become a Healer, and when it became obvious that Sara was never going to amount to that – or to any of the other prestigious jobs reserved for advanced ability witches – Heather became quite scathing to her daughter.

"Well, I am glad you've finally found something. Hopefully, you can move up the ladder from being a driver to something good."

"I enjoy what I do, mom," Sara said quietly. "I like being on my broom all day."

"Yes, of course you do. But work isn't always about what you like to do. Now, Tina. You wanted to ask me how you might go about becoming an Animal Healer?"

I nodded, grateful for the subject change. "Yes, please. I know it's a job that doesn't exist in the magical world, but it's the sort of thing I would really like to do. I thought a Healer might be the best person to give me guidance as to how I might go about it."

Heather nodded for a minute, thinking while Aurora came by with a tray laden with coffees and pastries. The coffees here were more like freakshakes – this one was bright pink, somehow, with marshmallow fluff around the rim, covered in whipped cream, sprinkles, and a glittering white chocolate unicorn horn. There was a reason it was only recommended to have one Hexpresso Bean coffee per day, and to me, that reason had more to do with the caloric content than the magical properties of the coffee.

"I would recommend that you take some beginner Healing classes, no matter what," Heather said. "I know they will be focused on healing paranormals rather than animals, but a lot of the basic healing principles I believe apply to living creatures of any kind."

"Oh," I said, my shoulders dropping slightly. "Isn't it super hard to qualify for entry into Healing classes?"

"It's difficult, but it certainly shouldn't be impossible if you're dedicated to it," Heather said. "The basic classes are a lot easier to get into than the advanced ones which you would require to become a Healer."

"Ok. So I still have a shot, then."

"Yes. I think the most difficult part would be learning about animals, and their specific healing. After all, there are no classes to teach you how to take care of them."

I nodded. "In the human world there are the non-magical equivalent of Animal Healers."

"In that case, I would recommend going to the human world and getting as many books as you can on the subject, and learning everything you can. That would be your next step after taking basic Healing classes."

"Ok," I nodded. "So I need to take basic Healing classes, and then learn about animal-specific anatomy as best I can."

"Exactly. Afterwards, I would see about taking more advanced Healing classes. You should have been a witch for long enough by then that you may get accepted, especially if you're as gifted a witch as Sara seems to think you are."

I blushed slightly. "Thanks. That's really kind of Sara to say."

"The most difficult part, I think, will be the transference of spells that we use for humans onto animals," Heather explained. "Your new job may require the creation of a number of new spells, which isn't easy. It would help if you knew what coven you were from, as it's always easier to perform your own coven's spells. To be honest, I would not recommend trying Jupiter's spells to try and save the life of an animal if you're not part of our coven. It's simply too risky."

My heart dropped in my chest. "Oh."

"Not to worry. I'm sure you'll discover which coven you're from eventually," Heather said with an encouraging smile. "This will be at least a year-long process for you. You will have plenty of time to overcome the more difficult obstacles while you tackle the easier ones."

"Thank you for the advice," I told her. "I really appreciate it."

"Of course. It's nice to see a young witch like yourself with so much ambition. I think becoming an Animal Healer is an excellent idea. And it's good to get some positivity today, what with everything else that's been going on."

"What do you mean, mom?"

Heather sighed as she looked at Sara. "I suppose it's going to be all over town later today anyway, but keep this to yourselves until then, all right?"

Sara and I nodded, our attention fixed on Heather.

"One of my colleagues performed the death test on Professor Lei this morning. It turns out she was murdered."

My hands rose to my mouth involuntarily as she said the words. So Ellie had been right.

"Murdered?" Sara whispered, barely audibly.

"That's right," Heather nodded. "She was whacked over the head with a heavy object."

"That can't be right," I chimed in. "I saw Professor Lei's body yesterday. There was no blood or anything like that. If she had been hit over the head, shouldn't it have looked a lot worse?"

"Not necessarily. In this case, the bleeding was all internal. It would have looked as though she simply fell over, but when in reality, she had absolutely been killed. The magic doesn't lie."

"Wow. So she really was murdered. It had to have been yesterday afternoon at some point, since Amy saw her a few hours before the exam," I mused.

"According to the doctor who examined the body, Professor Lei was killed within an hour of her body having been discovered. It's really quite tragic; I worked with Professor Lei a couple of times over the years. She was an excellent astronomist and mathematician. Her husband is one of the Healers at the hospital; I can't imagine how he's feeling right now."

"I remember Professor Lei," Sara said. "She was a hard teacher, but she was fair. She always gave me plenty of opportunity to improve my mark when my practical magic skills weren't as good as my theoretical ones."

"I can't believe somebody would want to murder someone from the coven," Heather said. "And to do it in coven headquarters as well. It's completely unheard of. I do hope they find Chief Enforcer King sooner rather than later so that she can get to the bottom of this."

Sara and I shared a look, and I nibbled at the cookie that Aurora had put in front of me. I didn't like this new development. Not one bit.

CHAPTER 6

Once Heather left, about five minutes later, Sara went to find Ellie, and convinced her that this was a great time to take her break. Ellie made her way over towards us and plonked herself down on a chair.

"What a crazy day," Ellie said. "I messed up a batch of the cookies earlier, and we only noticed because Andromeda took a bite of one, and started floating up to the ceiling. It was supposed to give the eater a feeling of floating, but it wasn't supposed to actually turn them into a living helium balloon. I came this close to having to call Amy to come over and fix my mistake, but at the last second I realized I had accidentally put in triple the amount of Pegasus feathers."

"So how did you fix it?" I asked.

"By quickly using a reverse levitation spell on

Andromeda," Ellie replied. "I knew it would reverse the effect of too many Pegasus feathers in the potion."

"Wow, that's crazy," I said.

"I don't even know how I did it. I must not have been paying attention. I was thinking about what might have happened to Chief Enforcer King."

"Well, on that note, that's why we called you out here," Sara said. "My mom was just here, and she said that it turns out Professor Lei was murdered."

"I knew it!" Ellie said triumphantly. "I knew she was too healthy to have just dropped dead out of the blue like that."

"She was hit over the head, and killed by internal bleeding," I explained. "You can't tell anyone until it's official, though."

"So who's investigating now that Chief Enforcer King isn't around?"

"I don't know," I said, turning to Sara. "Who would it be?"

"Well, my guess is it would be King's second-in-command. The Secondary Chief Enforcer," Sara mused.

"Ugh, not Orson Brown," Ellie said, making a face.

"Who's Orson Brown?" I asked.

"He's the second-in-command behind Aria," Ellie explained. "Have you ever heard of the idea that everyone rises to the level where they're incompetent, and then stayed there?"

"Of course, we call it the Peter Principle in the human world."

"Right. Well, Orson is the exception, in that he rose to his level of incompetence, and then kept going a few more rungs up the ladder. He's basically the most pompous idiot you'll ever come across, and he couldn't solve a mystery if the killer dropped into his lap."

"So how come he's the second-in-command in the Enforcer field?"

"His father is the head of the bear shifters. He continually pressed to have his son moved up the ladder in the Enforcer ranks, until he landed where he is."

"Was there a push to make him Chief Enforcer?" I asked.

"Oh, he pushed. So did his father. But you know Aria King," Ellie grinned. "She wasn't one to go down without a fight, and when it came down to it, the rest of the paranormals in town and the shifters all agreed that it was better to have someone actually competent in charge of law enforcement, so Orson missed out."

"And now he's in charge of a murder investigation *and* the disappearance of Chief Enforcer King, presumably," Sara said. "That basically means nothing is going to get discovered."

"Which is why *we* need to look into Professor Lei's death," Ellie said. "I know Amy thinks it's a terrible idea, but she's a part of our coven. We can't let a buffoon who doesn't deserve to carry a badge run this investigation."

"It's true there's no chance he'll come across the murderer," Sara said. "I'm up for investigating Professor Lei's death when I'm around. We owe it to her, as a member of the coven."

I nodded. "Same. I'm in. Hopefully, Chief Enforcer King will come back soon – I wonder what's happened to her."

"I don't think it's good," Ellie said ominously. "But who knows? I think we should focus on who killed Professor Lei, and let the Enforcers deal with Chief Enforcer King."

"Good plan," I said with a nod. "I agree."

"Same with me," Sara said. "Now, we just need to get Amy on board."

"That won't be too hard," Ellie grinned. "All we have to do is tell her that because of a murderer she won't be getting an exam mark for a while, and she'll be ready to lock up whoever did it herself."

I hid a smile. That certainly did sound like Amy.

"All right, so where do we start?" Sara asked. "After all, Tina and I have the rest of the afternoon off."

"Maybe we should see what we can find out about Professor Lei's day," I suggested. "We know she went to the town hall that day, maybe we can confirm what she went there to do."

"Good plan," Ellie said. "I'll see the two of you tonight back home."

With that, Ellie left, I sipped at the last bits of my coffee, and Sara nibbled at a corner of a cookie, looking pensive.

"I want to do right by her, Tina. Professor Lei was one of the few professors I had who actually seemed to care about my mark. Most of the professors, once they realized how bad I was at magic, figured I was a lost cause. They just ended up leaving me alone, since what was the point in teaching me anyway, my spells never worked right. But Professor Lei wasn't like that. Most of her classes were about theory rather than practical spells, but she still made sure that I had a chance to get a decent mark, and she actually tried to help me a lot more than most when it came to actually doing the spells right, too."

"Don't worry, we're going to find the person who did this," I said to Sara. "Or at least, we're going to do our best. Come on. Let's go see if we can find out what she was doing at city hall yesterday."

The two of us got up from our table and headed out, ready to start solving this new mystery.

~

*L*uckily for us, the main town hall wasn't too far from Hexpresso Bean, so it was a quick walk in the late-summer sunshine for us. I liked the town hall building. It was a whitewashed brick building, with awesome turrets, and a cute orange roof. Sara and I walked inside, where we were quickly met by a wolf shifter that I'd seen here before, working as a sort of security guard.

"Good afternoon, witches," the shifter said, looking us up and down. "What are you doing here today?"

"We're actually looking for the person who might have been working here yesterday," I said. "Was that you?"

"It was," the shifter replied with a curt nod. "Why are you asking about that?"

"We were wondering what Professor Lei was doing here," I answered. "We know she came here, we're simply trying to discover what for."

"I'm afraid I can't tell you that," the shifter replied, his eyes moving down the hall towards the office of Chief Enforcer King.

"She was here to see the Chief Enforcer, wasn't she?" I tried. After all, I was fairly certain that was correct.

"Um, I'm afraid that's, um, not my position to say."

"It's all right," Sara said with a disarming smile. "Let's say hypothetically, if Professor Lei had come here yesterday to see Chief Enforcer King, do you have any idea what it might have been about?"

"Hypothetically?" the wolf asked, his eyebrow rising.

"Of course," Sara smiled.

"Unfortunately, even hypothetically, I wouldn't have a clue. Hypothetically, if she came here yesterday, she just asked to see Chief Enforcer King, saying it was a private matter. She wouldn't tell me more. But hypothetically, that's not the first time."

"Really?" I said, my eyebrows rising. "She's come to see Chief Enforcer King before? Hypothetically, I mean."

The shifter nodded. "At least four times in the last two weeks, that I know of."

"Interesting. Thanks. And you have no idea where Chief Enforcer King is?"

He shook his head. "No. It's unlike her to be away for this long without telling anyone. Still, I'm holding my post. I hope she comes back soon, wherever she is."

"Do you think she might be hurt?" Sara asked. "We hope she's all right as well."

"I honestly don't know. Chief Enforcer King knows how to handle herself, that's for sure. But at the same time, this is so out of the ordinary for her, I don't know what to think. She's not invincible. She might be an incredibly strong and powerful shifter, but still. I know I'm hoping for her to be all right."

"We all are," I said quietly. "I hope she's found safe and sound sooner rather than later."

"Thanks," the shifter said with a small smile.

"Do you happen to know what she might have been working on?" Sara asked, but the shifter shook his head.

"I couldn't tell you if I did know, but the truth is I haven't got a clue. They always put rookies on the door watch, and I'm not high up in the hierarchy when it comes to being told what's going on."

"All right, thanks," I said, and Sara and I left.

"I wonder why she was seeing Chief Enforcer King so often," Sara mused.

"Me too. I wonder if Ellie isn't right about this, and the death and disappearance are linked."

"We need to find out what Professor Lei was seeing Chief Enforcer King about."

"It's too bad we can't get into her office."

"No, we can't. Not with the shifter around."

"You know where we might be able to go, though? Professor Lei's classroom."

Sara's eyes widened. "Do you really think that's a good idea?"

"Well, it might be. I mean, we won't look out of place in coven headquarters; we're witches."

"Ok, but I think we should wait until Ellie gets off work to do any real digging in places that might get us in trouble. I don't know how to do the spells to check for wards."

"Sure," I nodded. "We can definitely do that."

The two of us made our way towards coven head-quarters, and I couldn't help but wonder what on earth was going to come next.

## CHAPTER 7

About five minutes later Sara and I were at the entrance to the coven headquarters. We opened the door to find Amy at the entrance, watching those who entered.

"And what exactly are you two doing here?" she asked, her eyes narrowing.

"What, can't we visit our coven headquarters without getting the third degree from you?" Sara asked.

"Not when I know exactly what the three of you have probably been plotting."

"You're right," I said quickly. "We have actually decided to look into the murder."

Amy sighed. "I knew it. You guys, that's such an awful idea. That's what law enforcement is for."

"Yeah, except with Chief Enforcer King missing, that means Orson Brown is on the case," Sara explained. "Professor Lei was one of ours. We can't let her death go unsolved because of someone who should have been a buffoon shifter instead of a bear shifter being in charge of the investigation."

For the first time, I saw Amy's unwavering conviction slipping just a little bit, and I took advantage.

"Sara was telling me what Professor Lei meant to her. She was an important professor here, wasn't she?"

"She was," Amy said.

"And she taught you a lot, hasn't she?"

"That's right. A lot more than a lot of other professors."

"So, we just want to do right by her and her family. And her coven," I continued. "Come on. Help us make this right."

Amy sighed. "All right. Fine. But the *instant* Chief Enforcer King comes back, we're telling her everything we know and then staying out of it. Got it?"

Sara and I nodded. "Of course."

"Ok. What are you guys here for?"

"We're trying to find out what Professor Lei kept going to see Chief Inspector King about."

Amy raised her eyebrows. "You mean yesterday, when I saw her go into coven headquarters?"

"Yes, but it wasn't just then," Sara said, explaining to Amy what we had discovered just a few minutes earlier.

"Interesting," Amy said, mulling over the new information. "I hadn't heard about that at all."

"We were thinking of trying to get into her office to

see if we could get any information," I said. "But we were waiting for Ellie to get off work, first."

"You'll have to wait longer than that," Amy said, shaking her head. "The Enforcers are up there now. They got here about an hour ago. There's three of them. And I can't leave here until my shift is over."

"Didn't you just do an overnight shift working for Lita?" I asked, and Amy nodded.

"Yes, but I wanted to know if I could do another one. Distract the mind, and all. After all, now I don't know what's going to happen with the exam. Will there be another professor brought in who can give it shortly? Will the class be suspended? I have a lot of questions about my marks that Lita says are going to have to wait a few days, so I figured doing double time would be a decent distraction."

"Of course you'd be that worried about your grade," I laughed.

"Hey, it's important," Amy replied. "I need to get a good mark in that class."

"If there's Enforcers all around the office, I guess there's no real point in trying to get into Professor Lei's classroom, is there?" Sara asked.

Amy shook her head. "No, definitely not. There are a number of witches here, paying their respects, though. If you go to the prayer room down the hall, you may find someone who knows something."

"Thanks," I replied. "Are you coming with us?"

"No, I need to stay here. I am working, after all."

"Ok. We'll let you know what we find out," I said, and Sara and I made our way past Amy and into coven headquarters.

"Is the prayer room what I think it is?" I asked as Sara led me down the main part of the headquarters, towards where Lita's office was. However, we eventually made a left, towards a thick door with stained glass windows.

"Probably," Sara replied. "It's our room specially dedicated to the planet Jupiter, where witches from the coven can go for comfort and prayer whenever they feel the need to do so. It's also an informal meeting room to come together when there's a death in the coven. It's a calming place, where people can pay their respects."

I nodded. The prayer room did sound a lot like our churches back in the human world. Sara opened the door, and I gasped as I stepped past her and into the chapel.

This was really nothing like a church at all. Some sort of fog-like substance emanated from the ground, hiding everyone's feet. The walls had disappeared completely; instead we were all surrounded by a vision of space. It was like we were actually standing *in* Jupiter and its gasses, and were surrounded by space all around us.

I took a hesitant step forward, half expecting to fall through the floor and plummet through space forever, and instead found myself feeling almost weightless. It was sort of like being in the shallow end at the pool. I could still feel something that kind of felt like ground underneath my feet, but only barely, and I kind of half-jumped, half-floated from place to place.

Was this what being in space felt like?

I took a second to look at the walls around. Yes, this room was definitely designed to give the impression that we were floating through space. I could see Saturn, surrounded by its large rings, to my left, and a tiny Uranus over to my right. Wow.

"Are you ok?" Sara asked, leading me deeper into the room.

"Are we actually *on* Jupiter?" I asked, and Sara laughed.

"No. We're still very much on earth. But this room is enchanted to make us feel as though we're on our home planet, floating in the clouds of gas that make it up. It's calming, isn't it?"

"I wouldn't exactly say that," I muttered. This was way too weird to be entirely calming.

"Well, maybe if you were in the equivalent prayer room from your own coven you'd feel more comfortable," Sara replied. "Now come on, let's find some people to talk to."

Looking around, I noticed the other people for the first time. I'd been so focused on the fact that I literally felt like I was floating in space that I hadn't even realized there were about thirty people in this huge space.

A few witches were standing towards the edge of

the fog, sadly tossing handfuls of flower petals into the void. The petals floated away into space, and there was something oddly comforting about watching them. Others stood around the witches, watching the ritual.

To my right were some witches and wizards, standing together in a tight circle. They seemed to be speaking urgently about something, so I began to make my way towards them, trying to be subtle about it so I could maybe overhear what they were talking about.

Unfortunately, I completely forgot about the strange gravity in this room, and I quickly found myself careening towards the group, floating towards them in slow-motion but unable to stop myself.

"Excuse me, sorry!" I ended up calling out at the last second as I realized I was about to stumble straight into them. Most of the group got out of the way in time, but I hit an older wizard who didn't quite seem to have heard me in time. The two of us fell slowly into the fog, and a moment later I felt a hand around my elbow helping me up.

"Oh dear, you must be the new witch in town. I imagine you're not quite used to the gravity in here," a friendly-looking witch with curly dark blonde hair said as she helped me up.

"That's right. Thanks for the help. Sorry about that," I said to the older wizard, who was being helped up by another wizard.

"Watch where you're going next time, will you?" he harrumphed, scowling at me.

"Come on now, Elias. This is obviously that new witch in town; I'm sure this is her first time in a prayer room like this. It's Tina, isn't it?" the witch asked, and I nodded.

"That's right. I'm sorry about that. You're right, I've never been in anything quite like... this," I said, motioning around with my hands.

"Oh it's quite all right," the witch said. "I can only imagine how new this must all be for you. I'm Alex, one of the coven professors. And these are Elias, and John, two of the other professors as well."

"It's nice to meet you," I said. "Although I'm sorry it had to be under these circumstances."

"As are we," John said. He was tall, but rather on the stocky side. I would have expected him to be more of a rugby player or something than a professor. "Mai was a wonderful witch, and we're all going to miss her very much."

"I've only heard good things about her, and I hope whoever did this to her is found quickly," I said. The three professors exchanged glances.

"So it's making the rounds that she was murdered," Elias said quietly. "That poor witch, and her poor family. I can't imagine why anyone would have wanted to hurt her."

"Neither can I," John said, shaking his head. "Her poor family."

"I spoke to Andy this morning," Alex said, turning

to me. "That's her husband. He and the girls are just distraught."

"Do any of you know why she might have gone to see Chief Enforcer King yesterday?" I asked. After all, maybe Professor Lei had told some of her colleagues about her visits. But, the expressions on all three faces told me right away that no, they had no idea.

"I can't see why she would. She hadn't said anything to me about having problems with anyone."

"She had been acting a little bit strangely the last few weeks, though," John said pensively.

"Oh?" I asked.

"Yes. Going out a little bit more than usual. And at all hours; she was doing it in the middle of the day sometimes."

"That's right. She asked me to take over one of her classes last week," Alex said. "She told me she had to visit the Healers for a health issue she was dealing with."

That was interesting. Heather hadn't mentioned anything about Professor Lei needing a Healer, but maybe she didn't know? I made a mental note to talk to Sara about it.

"That was what she told me as well, when I asked," John said. "When I heard she'd died, I assumed that whatever she was dealing with was a lot more serious than she wanted anyone to know about it. But now that it's murder…" He trailed off, shaking his head sadly.

"She was a good witch, though," Elias said. "She deserves better than to have been killed in her own classroom. I do hope they find Chief Enforcer King sooner rather than later, and that she takes over this investigation, because there isn't a hope in Hades that Orson Brown will get anywhere."

"That's for sure," Alex muttered. "What an absolute disaster."

"I just hope Chief Enforcer King is all right," Elias said. "She's been the Chief Enforcer here for fifteen years, and she's always been reliable. She's much better than her predecessor was, that was for sure."

"And she's not afraid to ask for help when she needs it," John added. "Shifters can be so stubborn, but King isn't like that. I like her, and I hope she's found shortly as well."

"I do too," I said. "Well, I should get going. It was nice to meet you all."

"And you," Alex said with a smile. "If you ever get to the point where you'd like to learn about magical math, please feel free to enroll in one of my classes. I'm absolutely willing to give you some leeway based on your recent introduction to the magical community, and I think eventually getting a formal education would be good for you."

"Thank you," I said to her with a smile.

I made my way back towards Sara, mulling over what I'd heard. She was on the other side of the room now, speaking with a couple of witches near where the flower petals were being thrown into space.

This time, I was a little bit more prepared for the effects of the room as I made my way towards Sara. Before I reached her, however, my attention was caught by a couple of young witches speaking to each other nearby.

"You know, I can't believe she would do something like that."

"Don't you? Do you remember what happened to Anita after she got together with Richard?"

"Yeah, of course I do, but that doesn't mean that Kelly did this. There is a pretty big difference between casting an ugly spell on someone and murdering them."

Yes, eavesdropping on this conversation was a much better idea than making my way over towards Sara. I wondered who this Kelly they were talking about was.

"Sure, but isn't that how it starts? Someone who has a huge disrespect for another person's decisions might eventually turn to murder. Besides, I heard she was failing that class."

"Me too. Kelly told my sister that Professor Lei told her she needed to get at least ninety percent on that final exam for her average mark to be a passing grade."

"Well? What if she couldn't do it? I mean, we all know Kelly isn't exactly the shiniest wand in the pile. What do you think the odds are that she would've gotten ninety percent on a final exam in an advanced witch class?"

"I don't understand why Professor Lei even accepted her into that class," the first witch said. "After all, anyone who knows Kelly should've known that it was above her skill level."

"Her mother wants her to go into engineering," the other witch replied. "Her mom was telling my mom about it the other day. From what I heard, Kelly's mom put a significant amount of pressure on Professor Lei, and Lita, to let her into that class. I guess they eventually gave in, thinking that Kelly would fail and then she would never get to be an engineer anyway."

"Geez. I'm glad my mom doesn't care what I do. But still, do you really think Kelly has it in her to have killed Professor Lei?"

"I don't know," the other witch said slowly. "I mean, it is a jump to go from cursing someone to killing them, but then, you never know what someone will do when they get desperate enough."

"True. Well, I know that no matter what, I'm going to try not to get on her bad side anytime soon."

The two witches moved on, changing the topic to when the funeral might be, and I did the awkward half-jump half-walk towards Sara, who was just moving away from the crowd of people she was speaking to.

"You won't believe what I've heard," Sara said.

"And you won't believe what I've heard," I replied. "Want to get out of here and compare notes?"

"Yeah," Sara nodded, and we left the prayer room. I had to admit, as soon as I stepped over the door's threshold and back into a normal part of coven headquarters, I breathed a sigh of relief. Being in that fake space environment had a real creepy quality to it. I really wasn't entirely sure I was a fan.

Sara and I made our way back to the front of the building, only to find that Amy was busy talking with someone else. We waited for a couple of minutes, then decided to go home, waving at her as we went past. After all, Sara and I had some notes to compare.

## CHAPTER 8

"Ok, you go first," Sara said when we got back home. I plonked myself down on the couch and told her everything from my conversation with the professors, and the one I had overheard between the two witches.

"I assume you know the people involved better than I do?" I said, and Sara nodded.

"Yeah, for sure. Alex is Professor Alexandra Lyn. She teaches predominantly practical mathematics courses at the Academy. Her specialty overlapped with Professor Lei's quite a bit, so I'm not surprised she was there; the two of them would have worked pretty closely together quite a lot of the time."

"And Elias?"

"Professor Elias Blesk. I don't actually know him very well, he never taught me at all. I get the feeling he's not the nicest wizard, though. Actually, Professor

Lyn never taught me either. But I know her through my mom; they're kind of friends. Blesk is a potions professor, I think. But he mainly deals with the advanced classes. Amy will know him for sure. John… is he the short and thin John, or the tall John who looks like he spends all his free time working out?"

"The latter."

"Right. Then he's actually one of the spell-teaching professors. He deals with a lot of the younger students; Ellie, Sara, and I all had him as a Professor when we were teenagers."

"Let me guess, he was the Professor all the students had a crush on?" I said, and Sara grinned.

"You got it. One hundred percent. Ellie claims she managed to convince him to go out with her once, when we were seventeen, but none of us believed her."

"That does sound like the kind of story she would make up."

"That's interesting what they said about the Healers. I'll have to talk to my mom about it. I know the Healers all have a record to see who has been in for what that they can all access, just so that if there are any emergencies they can see exactly who has seen that paranormal before."

"And then there's this Kelly thing," I said. "Do you know who that is?"

"I don't know her, no. But then, I don't know a lot of the younger witches. We should wait for Amy to get home; she knows them all because she spends so much time at the Academy. Plus, it was one of the girls in her class, wasn't it?"

"Yeah," I nodded. "That's right. Because they said that she needed a really good mark to pass. Now, what was it that you found out?"

"Well, I was speaking with a witch who's one of Professor Lei's neighbors. She told me that a couple of nights ago, her husband Anthony left their house after a bit of a screaming match and didn't come back for a few hours afterwards."

"Did she know what the fight was about?"

"No, she said she could hear them yelling, but it was too far away for her to make out what they might have been fighting about."

"Ok. So it might have been nothing, but at the same time, it might not have. A couple of nights ago is awfully close to the time of the murder."

"That's what I thought, too."

"So we have three real avenues to look into," I said, ticking off my fingers as I went. "First, we have the potential medical issue. I can't really see what that might have to do with her death, since she was murdered, but I think we should look into it all the same as it was a behavior change in the weeks leading to her death."

"Right," Sara agreed.

"Next we have the husband. And finally, this Kelly witch."

"I think there might be a relatively easy way to find

out if the husband did it," Sara said. "After all, the entrances to the coven headquarters are all watched. It's done magically, and stored on a large scroll. Amy should be able to access it for us; I can text her. She'll be able to tell us everyone who was in the coven head-quarters when Professor Lei was killed."

"Excellent," I said, rubbing my hands together. "This might actually get us a solid lead or two. And better yet, it might even eliminate one of our suspects and help us focus a bit more."

Sara sent off the text, then kept tapping away at her phone. "I'm also going to ask my mom about what Professor Lei needed Healers for. That should answer that question for us, too."

"Good," I said with a smile. "Now, if that's it for now, I think I'm going to try and figure out what to do for my next movie night."

"Oh, you're going to keep doing that?" Sara said, her eyes lighting up. "Good! I liked the last movie you did."

My movie nights were my small way of trying to bring the different paranormal communities together. I didn't like the segregation that seemed to dominate the paranormal world, and I wondered if using something everyone could love – in this case, movies from the human world – couldn't help bridge that gap.

"*Spice World*?" I said with a grin. "Yeah, that's a great movie. I was thinking I would stick with stand-alones for a little bit, since I want to bring people in. No one is going to want to come start off watching *Star Wars* with the fourth movie."

"Good plan," Sara nodded. "Any movie in mind?"

"Maybe *Dodgeball*," I replied. "That's got some memorable lines, and it's really funny. It's kind of an older movie now, but of course, no one here even knows that, since no one in Western Woods watches human movies anyway. I'm going to text Kyran, and try to get him to get me a copy."

"All right," Sara nodded as I grabbed my phone off the table and began to text him. Kyran was an elf who lived somewhat in exile from the rest of the residents of Western Woods. His self-determined job kept him travelling in the human world extensively, which meant that he was the perfect person to send to find me DVDs I could use for my displays.

*Hey, next time you're in the human world can you get me a DVD of Dodgeball?*

I tried not to keep my eyes glued to the phone waiting for an answer. After all, Kyran had his own life. He almost certainly wasn't sitting around staring at his phone, waiting for me to text him to ask a favor. Still, as my phone dinged to indicate a reply, my heart skipped a beat.

*Sure. I'll come by later with it.*

Heat rose to my face involuntarily as I read the reply. Nope. I was totally not going to get involved with someone this soon after moving to Western

Woods. Besides, I was a witch. I didn't even know if inter-species relationships were *allowed* here.

Nope. I was definitely *not* going to let myself be into Kyran. I was doing all right for myself on my own. There was no need to ruin it by bringing a man into the picture. Kyran and I were just friends, and that was how it was going to stay.

Before I had a chance to get further into my own head, however, Amy came into the room.

"Shift over?" Sara asked, and she nodded.

"Yeah. Did you guys find out anything interesting?"

Sara and I recounted everything we had discovered in the prayer room.

"Do you know who this Kelly might be?" I asked, and Amy nodded.

"For sure. That sounds exactly like Kelly Treach. She was in that class, you would have seen her there yesterday. One of the girls who was crying in the corner."

"Maybe she was crying because she knew she'd done something awful, not because she was upset about a death," Sara offered. "What do you know about her?"

"She's annoying, a terrible witch, and she should never have been accepted into that class in the first place," Amy said. "Frankly, I feel like having allowed her in there was detrimental to everyone else's learning, since she was constantly interrupting and talking about stuff that had nothing to do with our assigned topics."

"So the witches weren't wrong, the class was above her skill level?"

"Absolutely," Amy said. "Once I traded papers with her when we did a quiz; she got forty-five percent on it. I can't imagine why Lita would have let her into that class."

"Well, pressure from her mom, no doubt. It's hard, you guys, when your parents have expectations for you that you have no chance of being able to meet," Sara said softly.

"I know," Amy said. "All the same, it is no excuse for murder. You never would have killed a professor to get out of an exam."

"Only because I knew you would have killed me in retaliation," Sara shot back. "Ok, maybe that's not entirely true. You are right that I never would have done something like that. I just never pushed when I wasn't accepted into advanced classes, because I knew I didn't belong there. And luckily, I think my mom knew that as well."

"Right. So she's definitely a suspect," I said. "She would have been in the coven headquarters at the time of the murder. Speaking of, Amy, did you bring the list with you?"

Amy nodded. "Obviously, I couldn't bring the list itself," she said. "I did, however, copy down the names and entry times of everyone who entered coven head-quarters that day."

"Does the list cover when people left, as well?" I asked, but Amy shook her head.

"No. Only when they enter."

"All right," I said. "Let's see it."

"It's a long list," Amy warned as she took a small notebook from her pocket and handed it over to me. Sara got up and made her way towards me, and I pushed the notebook between us so we could both read the names at once. I started off by flipping the pages to see just how long the list was, and as I kept flipping and flipping, my heart sank.

"There have to be at least a hundred names here."

"I told you, there were a lot of people who went through headquarters," Amy said with a shrug.

"All right. So the first person to go through the doors this morning was Lita," I said. "Then there's a few other names here I don't recognize."

Sara and I scanned through the list. It seemed like half the coven – and a bunch of non-witches – all made their way into coven headquarters that day. I saw a bunch of names I didn't recognize, and some that I did. Patricia Trovao, who worked at the hospital, had come in early that morning. Lita's name appeared three or four times, and there was Heather Leach. John came in late in the morning, and Alex a couple of hours later. Amy's name appeared an hour before the exam was about to start. About four pages in, however, as I read one of the names just below Amy's, I let out a bit of a triumphant cry.

"There!" Pointing to one of the names on the list, Amy and Sara both looked forward to see what I had noticed.

*Yao Lei – 3:47pm*

"So her husband came into coven headquarters about an hour before she was killed," Amy mused. "Interesting."

"I wish we knew what that argument they had was about," Sara said. Just then, her phone beeped and she looked at the screen.

"My mom says that Professor Lei hadn't seen a Healer in over six months," Sara continued, her features folding into a frown. "So why would she tell people that was where she was going?"

"Could the information be wrong? Could she have seen a Healer without it being recorded?"

Sara shook her head. "No, Healers are required to report every single patient they see, and their information. It's one of the most important parts of being a Healer in the paranormal world, and any Healer who saw a patient without recording the visit would be sanctioned harshly."

"So she was lying to her coworkers about what she was doing," Amy mused. "And at the same time, we know she was going to the town Hall. We know she was visiting Chief Enforcer King."

"I think we need to figure out what it was Chief

Enforcer King was working on," I said. "It might be nothing, but I wouldn't be surprised if the murder and the disappearance have something to do with one another."

"Okay, so how do we go about that?" Amy asked. "After all, it's not like we're just going to be able to go into coven headquarters and look through her things."

"Maybe Kyran will be able to help," I said. "After all, he's coming over later today with a DVD for my next movie in the park."

"So we wait for him," Amy nodded. "That works for me."

"While you're working at coven headquarters, you should also try to find out what you can about Professor Lei and her marriage," Sara suggested to Amy. "After all, I don't think we should write off the husband just yet, especially seeing as he came into the building less than an hour before Professor Lei was killed."

"Okay," Sara agreed. "We're going to tackle this from a few different angles, and hopefully we can narrow down exactly why Professor Lei was killed."

## CHAPTER 9

*A* few hours later Ellie came back home, and we kept her up to date with what we had discovered.

"Crazy. I never would have imagined that Professor Lei would have so much going on that there would be multiple people out there who might want her dead," Ellie said, shaking her head.

"Hopefully Kyran will have some information for us," I said. As if right on cue, all of a sudden there was a knock at the front door, and I stood up to get it. "That'll be him now."

I made my way to the front of the house, and as soon as I opened the door I beamed at the elf in front of me. Kyran almost looked like way too much of a bad boy to be an elf. He certainly didn't look like Orlando Bloom or Hugo Weaving in *The Lord of the Rings*. Instead, his short brown hair was cut somewhat regularly and gave him a permanent just got out of bed look, and his eyes were as blue as ice on a glacier.

"Hey, how's it going?" I asked.

"Yeah, good. Mind if I come in for a minute?"

I pulled the door open and stepped aside to let Kyran come past.

"Did you manage to find the DVD?"

"I did, eventually. Why can't you just embrace modern movies like most humans? If you wanted *Thor* or *The Avengers* it would have been way easier to get a hold of."

"Yeah, well, those movies don't have amazing lines like "if you can dodge a wrench, you can dodge a ball"."

"Fair enough," Kyran laughed, handing me the disk.

"Hey, while you're here, I'm wondering if I can ask another favor from you?"

"Go for it," Kyran said.

"I was wondering if you'd be able to find out for us what Chief Enforcer King is working on right now."

Kyran frowned. "Why do you want to know?"

"We think it might be related to Professor Lei's death, which we're kind of looking into, since apparently Orson Brown is a total idiot who wouldn't be able to catch a bank robber if he handed him a wad of hundred dollar bills."

"Yeah, that makes sense. Orson is an idiot. There isn't a chance in hell you're going to get any sort of answers with him in charge. But I'm sorry, I can't go find out that information for you."

My heart sank in my chest. "Oh, cool," I said, trying not to show my disappointment. After all, Kyran didn't actually owe me anything. If anything, I owed him for a whole bunch of favors.

"It's nothing to do with you," Kyran replied. "I promise. I would do this for you if I thought it wouldn't affect you at all."

"What do you mean? Is there a reason why we should stop looking into Chief Enforcer King's disappearance?"

Kyran shook his head. "No, it's nothing like that."

"Okay. Well, thanks for the DVD," I said, holding up the disk.

"No problem. Sorry I can't help you. What I can tell you though, is that the shifter switch for shifts takes place at midnight, and if I were going to try and sneak into Chief Enforcer King's office, that's the time I would pick, since things are a little bit more hectic than they are at other times of the day," Kyran added with a wink.

"Thanks," I smiled. "I appreciate the heads up."

As Kyran left, however, I couldn't help but feel like something was a little bit wrong. I wasn't sure what, but there was definitely something. It just felt off. Kyran was normally super happy to help, and if not, he wasn't invasive about the reasons why. I wondered what on earth was going on.

Making my way back into the living room, I shared

the new information that I had gathered with the others.

As I finished, Amy groaned. "This means the rest of you are going to want to break into the City Hall, doesn't it?"

"Of course," Ellie grinned. "It sounds like that's going to be the best way to find out what Chief Enforcer King was working on."

"And of course, you guys know that I'm not going to let you do it by yourselves, since I'm the best of the four of us at finding wards, and we all know that Chief Enforcer King's office is going to be warded to the hilt."

"Isn't it nice having friends that manage to guilt you into having adventures?" Ellie replied.

"You say adventures, I say felonies."

"Po-tay-to, po-tah-to," Ellie grinned, earning herself a glare from Amy.

"Okay, so if everybody agrees that this is the thing we're actually going to do, when should we do it? I think tonight would be best; I want to get to the end of this as quickly as possible," I chimed in.

"I agree," Ellie said. "After all, the sooner we managed to figure out exactly why someone killed Professor Lei, the more likely we are to actually find the killer. I'd rather know sooner rather than later whether we're on the wrong track with this."

"I agree," Sara said.

"All right," Amy nodded. "It's settled then. Lita told

me to go home and get some rest, so I'm not working tonight either."

It looked like once again, the four of us were going to make a middle of the night break in to try and get some information.

The difference was, this time we were well and truly going into the belly of the beast. We were trying to get information on the head of law enforcement in town.

$\sim$

*B*y 11:30, the four of us were standing by the front door, getting ready to leave.

"I don't understand why I can't come," Mr. Meowgi complained. "After all, only the vampires and some of the shifters can see me in the dark anyway. Besides, the last time you did this, if it wasn't for me, you wouldn't have even gotten into the building."

It was true that Mr. Meowgi's black coat was definitely an advantage in the middle of the night. And he did have a point about having come in handy the last time.

"Fine," I relented. "You can come, but you have to stay out of the way. And if you see a shifter who might be able to see you in the dark, you definitely need to stay away."

"I have the subtlety and agility of a ninja; you don't need to worry about me."

Somehow, I wasn't convinced.

"We're going to walk," Ellie said. "I think it will be the best way to go; it's early enough that we could very well be going to The Magic Mule for a couple of late-night drinks."

"Good plan," Amy chimed in. "Since the bar is just around the corner from City Hall, we'll be heading the right way anyway, so we'll have a built-in excuse if anyone asks us what we're doing."

"Mr. Meowgi is coming with us as well," I added. Sara reached down and gave him a pat on the head.

"I hope you're ready for an adventure little guy," she told him.

"I was born ready," Mr. Meowgi replied to her, even though she couldn't understand him. I smiled; while all the other girls familiar's were happy to hang around in the house all the time - except for Amy's owl who liked to fly around on his own at night - it was kind of nice to have a cat who enjoyed coming with me wherever I went.

Our whole crew left the house and began making our way down to the center of town. We were all dressed normally, which was kind of strange given what our plan was, but it would have looked a lot more suspicious if we were all dressed in black as we made our way down for what was supposed to be a casual drink at the local witch's bar.

Ten minutes later we reached City Hall, and quickly made our way towards a bench that overlooked the river that snakes through town. After all, from here we would look like just a crowd of witches getting ready to go in for a drink, rather than a group of witches planning on breaking into Chief Enforcer King's office.

"Okay, what do we do to start?" Sara asked. "There are a lot more people here than I was expecting."

Sure enough, there were still a few shifters, vampires, and witches meandering through the streets. We were going to either have to use an invisibility spell on ourselves or do something else if we planned on getting in without being seen.

"Why don't we send Mr. Meowgi in?" I asked. "After all, no one is really going to think too much of a cat wandering around."

"Of course I'm willing to go be a scout," Mr. Meowgi said, looking excited at the prospect of being involved. "The four of you stay here; I'll be back soon with any information to report about who is inside the building."

As he darted off towards the town hall, I explained to the others what was going on, and we stood around nonchalantly, waiting for my familiar to return with his report.

Mr. Meowgi returned about five minutes later, looking extremely pleased with himself.

"Right. Something is definitely happening in there, all of the shifters are moving around instead of just standing at their posts. Everyone seems tense for some reason, too. Once you're inside Town Hall, however, there isn't much to deal with until you've reached Chief Enforcer King's office. It's going to be slipping past the shifter at the door that's going to be your issue, since both shifters are wolves with a keen sense of smell."

"Okay, so both of the guards are wolf shifters, which means we can't go invisible?"

"That's right," Amy nodded. "It's unfortunate; if the guards had been lion shifters or bear shifters instead, we wouldn't have had a problem with an invisibility spell, but wolf shifters are hard. Even if we go invisible, they're going to be able to sniff our presence."

"What we need is a distraction," Ellie said. She looked over at Mr. Meowgi, who practically beamed as the realization dawned upon him that he was going to be called on to help once more.

"Of course, I can cause a distraction," Mr. Meowgi bragged. "Obfuscation is an important skill for every martial artist such as myself to master."

"Great, if you're in then that means Amy can cast the invisibility spell on all of us, and then we can slip into the building while you distract the wolf shifter guard." I said.

"Everybody ready?" Amy asked. "Once we get past the guard, we meet in front of Chief Enforcer King's office. Nobody try to go in before I have a chance to check for wards, since it's almost certain that there will be protection of some kind on the door to her office."

The three of us nodded, and a moment later Amy

took out her wand, looked around to make sure there was nobody checking to see what we were doing, and cast the invisibility spell. While most witches had to chant the incantation to go with this spell, Amy was an advanced enough witch that she managed to do so silently. It was pretty strange, a moment later, when Sara suddenly disappeared, and only seconds later, I looked down to see that I had completely disappeared as well.

## CHAPTER 10

*W*hen all four of us were invisible, Mr. Meowgi ran back towards the City Hall entrance. I followed after him this time, making sure to stay at least twenty feet away from the door, hoping that was far enough away to avoid arousing suspicion by the wolf shifter guard.

About five seconds later, I heard a crash, and then a shout. "What on earth was that? Hey! Get back here!"

Daring to step a little bit further forward, I poked my head into the building to see the guard rushing after Mr. Meowgi, away from the door.

Perfect.

I slipped into the building and began speed walking down the hall towards Chief Enforcer King's office. I refused to turn to look behind me; if I didn't know what was back there, then I couldn't be caught. At least, that was the reasoning my brain was going for. Making a beeline towards the office door, I stopped when I reached it.

"You guys here?" I whispered.

"Yup," Sara's voice replied a moment later.

"Same here," Ellie said.

"Amy?" I asked quietly, looking around.

"Yeah," Amy replied, sounding slightly out of breath. "I made it. Let me check the door for wards."

She muttered a spell under her breath, and a second later, the door glowed green. However, it glowed a much deeper green than the last time I had seen Amy do this same spell.

"This isn't an easy ward to break," Amy muttered, and I could hear the frustration in her voice. Still, none of us had expected this office to be an easy one to break into. For a few moments, I heard Amy muttering spells, then re-doing the ward test. The first three times, the door glowed green once more. But on the fourth try, nothing happened.

"Good, we're in," Amy said, and the door handle seemed to turn by itself before the door swung open. "I'm going to check for wards inside really quickly. Stay outside until I tell you."

I held my breath while Amy muttered a spell once again, but when she finished, nothing glowed.

"Ok, we're good to go."

I slipped into the room along with the others, bumping into someone – I wasn't quite sure who – along the way.

"Sorry," I whispered.

"No problem," Ellie whispered back.

"Everyone in?" Amy asked, and after a murmur of assent from all of us, the door closed.

"Can you reverse the invisibility spells for a while?" Ellie asked. "After all, if one of the shifters come in here, they're going to be able to sniff us out."

"Fine," Amy said, and one by one the four of us re-appeared, with Amy making herself visible last. I looked down at my hands like I'd never seen them before; I still wasn't entirely used to this whole invisibility thing.

"Ok," Ellie said, making her way over to Chief Enforcer King's desk. "Time to get cracking, ladies. Let's try and be out of here in the next five minutes."

I immediately saw Ellie grabbing at some stuff on the desk, and I made my way to a cabinet along the side wall. Opening it, I found a book filled with expense reports.

It appeared Chief Enforcer King had eaten at various restaurants. "Chief Enforcer King sure liked eating at Elixir of Life," I commented out loud. "What is that place?"

Ellie looked at me strangely. "Really? When?"

"Umm, she's billed them four times in the last month," I said, scanning the expense report. "Why?"

"Elixir of Life is a bar in one of the towns near here," Ellie explained. "I'm surprised to hear that Chief Enforcer King would have to go there so often, seeing as she is Chief Enforcer here are not there, but at the same time Desert Plains isn't exactly the best paranormal town."

"I think that was her main case," Sara said, going through her papers. "She's obviously been doing a whole bunch of research about the gambling and the kinds of paranormals that have been heavily involved in that."

"Interesting," Amy said. "Maybe that was what Professor Lei was helping her with? After all, she was predominantly an astronomy professor, but she also did teach a few math courses."

"I have a few meetings here on the calendar between Chief Enforcer King and some names I don't recognize," Ellie said, grabbing a Post-it note and jotting the names down. "I think we should look into this thing she was doing in Desert Plains, since it sounds like it was her main case."

"Good," Amy said. "Now, let's get invisible again, and get out of here as fast as we can."

A few minutes later, the four of us were invisible and standing outside of Chief Enforcer King's office once more.

"How are we going to get past the guard now?" I asked. "After all, if he can smell us, then he is going to be able to smell us when we leave too, right?"

"Right," Amy said. "At least it's easier to cause a distraction from the inside. When I say run, run. We'll all meet at the side of The Magic Mule."

"Got it," Ellie said. I waited with bated breath, curious as to what Amy was about to do, when a few minutes later the acrid smell of smoke reached my nostrils, and I heard shouts coming from towards the main doors.

"Crap, how on earth did that tapestry catch fire?" I heard the guard asked as he sprung up from his chair and rushed towards the back wall of the building.

"Now, run," Amy said, and I didn't need to be told twice. I rushed towards the front door like I was an Olympic sprinter competing for a gold medal. Even though it was less than one hundred feet, I'd exerted so much effort that by the time I reached the sidewalk, I was panting for breath. I stopped and put my hands on my knees for a second before rushing towards The Magic Mule, not wanting to be near the entrance to the town Hall for any longer than was strictly necessary.

By the time I got there, Amy had made everybody else visible again. A second later, after announcing my arrival, I was visible once more as well.

"So? What did you witches find out?" Mr. Meowgi asked.

"I'll let you know once we get home," I said. "I don't want to talk about it in public."

I was fairly certain we'd discovered which case was taking up most of Chief Enforcer King's time these days. I was also pretty sure we were going to have to go visit Desert Plains.

~

*T*he next morning, Sara had to go to work, and Amy had to go to coven headquarters for a meeting of all the students who had their exam not take place due to Professor Lei's murder. That left Ellie and I available for the day to go visit Desert Plains and see what information we could dig up.

"Make sure to interview Kelly," Ellie said. "After all, she is one of our main suspects, and it would be interesting to see what she has to say about Professor Lei."

"I will," Amy nodded. "If we're lucky, by the end of the day we'll hopefully be able to narrow down our suspect list to just a few people."

I sincerely hoped Amy was right. By the time Ellie and I were the only two people left in the house, I realized that I was actually a little bit nervous.

"So are all paranormal towns like Western Woods?" I asked Ellie.

She shook her head. "No, they can actually all be quite different. For example, not all paranormal types live in all towns. Here in Western Woods, we have witches, vampires, fairies, elves, and shifters. That's pretty standard for most of the towns based in America. However, if you were to go to Europe, you would find the town makeups to be quite different. Eastern Europe has a very heavy vampire influence, Northern Europe has quite a few more fairies than most other places, Iceland's paranormal towns are almost entirely comprised of elves, and some places have different paranormals that we don't even have. In Greece, for example, the paranormal towns have nymphs, but you would never find a bear shifter there."

"Interesting," I said. "So really, even the paranormal world is a lot like the human world, where different parts of it have different populations."

"Exactly. When we get to Desert Plains, you'll find that it looks significantly different to Western Woods, but the population makeup will be fairly similar."

"How do we get there? Are we going to go see Drake?" Drake was a dragon shifter who guarded the tree that was used to get back to Seattle.

Ellie shook her head. "No, to get to other paranormal towns there is actually a special portal, since there are so many of them, and travel between paranormal towns is much more common than travel between the paranormal world and the human world."

"Cool," I said, but in reality, I was a little bit nervous. Everything about Western Woods had been so new, this was definitely going to be taking things to a whole new level. As if she could read my mind, Ellie gave me a gentle smile.

"Don't worry. There's nothing to be afraid of. It's no worse than travelling between the human world and the paranormal world. Besides, I'll be with you the whole time."

"Thanks," I said to her with a kind smile. If there was anyone I would be comfortable going somewhere completely new with, I had to admit, it was definitely Ellie. She was just so incredibly street smart; she was the type of witch who could get by absolutely anywhere.

"Good," she said. "Now, let's get going. We have a lot of stuff to figure out."

aking a deep breath, I steeled myself as we arrived at the portals leading to the other paranormal towns. I wasn't sure what exactly I had been expecting, but it wasn't this. I found myself staring at a short line that seemed almost airport-security-like. A shifter – I couldn't exactly make out what type, but her deep eyes and long, blonde hair made me think possibly another dragon shifter – stood at the front of the line, asking questions and searching bags before sending people towards a huge tree stump. The stump had to be at least twenty feet wide, and as soon as the person she had been helping stepped on it, he disappeared.

I let out a gasp as the shifter was replaced with a shimmer of deep red light for a split second before that disappeared as well.

"Next!" the dragon shifter called out, and a fairy

made her way up towards the guard, showing her purse.

"So is it common for people from Western Woods to travel to other paranormal towns?" I asked Ellie, turning towards her.

"Fairly common, yes. A lot of paranormals travel for work, or to visit family. After all, some paranormal's choose to leave their coven and join a new one when they find somebody they've fallen in love with."

"So this line isn't out of the ordinary at all?"

"No. You'll find that it moves fairly quickly though; I've never had to wait more than five minutes to enter the portal to a different town."

"Does it take a long time? Or is it like the oak tree to Seattle where the transfer is almost instant?"

"It's instant," Ellie said, tilting her head slightly. "Why wouldn't it be?"

"Well, back in the human world, if I wanted to travel to say, Australia, it would take a fifteen hour flight before I could get there."

Ellie's mouth dropped open. "That's barbaric!"

I shrugged. "Well, there really aren't any other options right now in the human world."

"If you ever decide you do want to visit Australia, let me know. We'll go for a few days," Ellie said with a grin. I shook my head with disbelief. I couldn't believe that here in the paranormal world, I was literally only seconds away from being able to visit anything on the planet that I wanted to.

I made a mental note to start researching cool vacation locales. After all, it wasn't like I had travelled very much in my life. My parents took me to Disneyland one year, but that was basically it. Maybe I could go to Paris, or somewhere warm like the Bahamas.

My impromptu vacation planning took a backseat, however, as Ellie and I found ourselves quickly approaching the front of the line, just as Ellie had said we would.

"Next!" the shifter barked, and Ellie nudged me forward.

"Come on, I'll go with you," she said, and the two of us made our way towards the shifter.

"You know the rules, one at a time," the shifter said with a glare towards the pair of us.

"This is the new witch in town, she has no idea how to use the portal," Ellie explained quickly.

The shifter looked me up and down. "So you're the new witch. Well, rules are rules. Step back," she continued, ordering Ellie to move behind.

"She needs help," Ellie replied, holding firm.

"Well, let me put it this way. If you don't step back right now, neither one of you is going to make it to your destination today."

Evidently, the fact that I had no idea how magic worked compared to the other people who lived here was not going to make a difference to this shifter. Her blue eyes really were as cold as ice; they matched her interior perfectly.

"It's okay, Ellie," I said as I saw my friend open her mouth to argue once more. "I can handle this on my own."

I had no idea whether or not that was true.

"Where are you going today?" The shifter asked, holding out a hand.

"Desert Plains," I replied. "I don't have a purse, sorry, I don't know what you're asking for me."

"Your wand, obviously," the shifter replied, like it was the most obvious thing in the world.

"Sorry," I muttered sheepishly as I took my wand out of my pocket and handed it over. The shifter looked it over, tapping it carefully against the back of her hand, before handing it back. Evidently, whatever test my wand had just gone through, it had passed.

"Right, move along then."

"What do I do?" I asked. "I've never done this before."

The shifter let out a deep sigh, like my innocent question was the most annoying thing she had ever heard. But, a moment later, she answered. "You just go up and stand on the log there. I've already entered your destination, so all you need to do is step onto it and the portal will transport you to Desert Plains automatically."

"Okay, thanks," I muttered, looking over at the log which suddenly seemed a lot more intimidating than it had only a few moments ago. What if something went wrong? What if the shifter entered the wrong paranormal town, and I ended up somewhere completely different?

I pushed those thoughts to the back of my head. After all, that was totally not going to happen. While it was new to me, it was obvious the paranormals were totally used to this method of transport, which meant nothing was going to go wrong.

Right?

I stepped up onto the log, and realized I genuinely had no idea what to expect next. About a second after I stepped onto it, I felt a whoosh in my ears, and a drop. This was definitely different to the portal that took me back to Seattle. This portal felt more like I was dropping through a water slide but without any water, with blackness around me, and no idea where the ending was. As soon as it started, however, the feeling dissipated and I found myself standing on solid ground once more.

I opened my eyes to find that I was on top of a pyramid, looking over a vast desert. I could see the horizon in every direction without any problem, and it looked like everything here was made from a deep yellow sand. To my left, a large number of scattered buildings reminded me of those towns from old Western movies. They were all made of wood, and were mainly low-lying. They were pretty far away though, so I couldn't make out much more than that.

"Hey! You!" someone called out to me. I looked around to see a bear shifter motioning over towards me. "Get off the arrivals pad, you're holding up the line!"

"Sorry!" I squeaked, looking towards the shifter. Next to him was a set of stairs that led down to the bottom of the pyramid, and I made my way towards them and stepped off the small peak of the pyramid.

The instant I stepped off it, Ellie appeared where I had been standing a moment before. She grinned at me as soon as she looked over to see me, and made her way over.

"See? Nothing to worry about."

"All right, witches, let's move it along," the shifter said. "This is one of the busiest portals in this part of the paranormal world, we can't have you here wasting time. Make your way to the bottom of the pyramid and you'll find a chariot that will drive you to town."

I made my way down the steps of the stone-hewn pyramid, and as soon as Ellie and I reached the ground, a golden chariot appeared in front of us. It moved as though by magic, and it took me a second to realize that was exactly how it moved.

"All right, get in," Ellie said to me, and I hopped into the chariot, the temperature dropping at least fifteen degrees as soon as I stepped into it. It was nice; I hadn't realized just how hot it was outside until I stepped into the small box.

"This is pretty nice," I said as Ellie followed me in, and as soon as she closed the chariot door behind her, it began to move silently along the ground towards town. I looked out over the desert, enjoying the view through the chariot window. I had never seen anywhere like this before.

"Desert Plains is really nice," Ellie confirmed. "It gets really hot here, but it's a dry heat, so it's very manageable. Of course, right now, since it's not the middle of summer, it's a little bit cooler than it can get."

"So what do you think Chief Enforcer King was doing here?" I asked. "I know I haven't been to the town yet, but from the view I got from the pyramid I assume it's kind of like the seedy underbelly of the paranormal world?"

Ellie laughed. "Okay, it's sort of seedy, especially if you go to the wrong part of town. But for the most part Desert Plains is like the entertainment capital of this part of the paranormal world. You'll see when you get there. It doesn't look like much from the outside, but as soon as you get in and see what's happening you'll know what I mean."

"So it's sort of like paranormal Vegas?"

"Las Vegas is the closest human town, yes. The overall tone here is different though. Gambling is a major part of the life here, but there isn't as much outward glitz and glamour as you would find in Las Vegas. And there definitely is an underground here. I suspect we're going to have to get involved in that side of things to figure out what Chief Enforcer King was doing here."

I nodded as I looked out the window, and realized

that the chariot had basically already brought us into town. As I looked out the window, I realized that the initial impression I'd had was correct – it looked exactly like we were driving through the middle of a western. The buildings around were all made of old distressed wood, the road was paved but covered in a thin layer of dust that seemed to dominate, and even the signs advertising mainly gambling and drinking were old-fashioned.

"Where do we start?" I asked. "And where is the chariot going to drop us off?"

"That's the beauty of these chariots," Ellie said with a grin. "They're magical. They take you exactly where you need to go. For most people, that's a hotel. But for us, we have other plans."

A second later, the chariot ground to a stop.

"Here we are," Ellie said. "This is exactly where we need to go, even if we don't know it yet."

I stepped out of the chariot and found myself facing one of the most incredible buildings I had ever seen in my life.

CHAPTER 12

*I*t could have been something straight out of an old movie. We were on the corner, looking at a whitewashed wooden building, with a huge balcony that wrapped around both sides of the building. Large windows that were almost floor to ceiling height gave us a look in where groups of witches and wizards were obviously enjoying some drinks. The sign above the door read *The Witch's Brew*.

Vintage Edison bulbs lit up the space from the outside, and while the floorboards creaked under our feet as Ellie and I made our way to the front door, it was obvious that they were sturdy and good quality, and I had a feeling that the creaking was more magical than the owner would like to admit.

The bar's interior had an amazing farmhouse style look that would make any Etsy-loving interior designer proud. Hardwood floors, a bar at the back made with reclaimed barn doors, wrought-iron stools with wooden tops covered in rawhide, succulents lining empty spaces and long tables made of reclaimed wood gave the space an incredibly intense atmosphere. Vintage bulbs hung from the ceiling, casting a warm glow over the space.

That, however, was where the warmth ended. The groups of people enjoying their drinks huddled together, none of them paying any attention to Ellie or me. Behind the bar was a single wizard, currently busy waving his wand at a cloth on the counter that danced along it, cleaning as it went. Instead of welcoming us, however, the bartender looked at us like he was trying to figure out what we were about.

Ellie walked straight up to the counter, and I followed her lead.

"Two vodka, straight," Ellie ordered, and the bartender nodded at her before waving his wand at a couple of bottles on the wall. "No, not those ones. We want the good stuff."

Ellie obviously knew what she was doing. Seeing as I definitely didn't, I kept my mouth shut, and tried to look confident like I totally knew what she was on about. The bartender grunted and pointed his wand at two different bottles, which shot out from the wall and poured themselves into two waiting shot glasses. The shot glasses slid across the table, one towards each of us.

Luckily, years of working in a bar meant that I

knew exactly how to down a shot and look cool while doing it. I grabbed the shot and downed it in one gulp, slamming the shot glass back down on the table. Ellie did the same, giving me a subtle look to show she was impressed by how well I'd done it.

"Right," Ellie said when she finished. "You haven't had any shifters in the bar lately, have you?"

The bartender looked at her suspiciously. "Who's asking? This is a witch and wizarding bar, isn't it?"

"Yeah, well, I'm looking for the shifter that was here a few times. Lion. Not from here."

"Why should I tell you anything?"

Ellie reached into her pocket and pulled out an envelope I didn't realize she had. She slipped it over to the bartender, who pulled out a wad of abracadollars, the magical currency. His eyebrows rose.

"So what if I've seen her?"

"What was she here for?"

"It wasn't drinking, if that's what you're asking," the wizard replied, his eyes narrowing.

"And a completely aboveboard establishment like this one wouldn't have any unlicensed gambling going on, would it?" Ellie asked, her eyes narrowing.

"Of course it wouldn't," the man replied, looking insulted.

"So if I wanted to get involved in a little bit of duel betting, where would I go for that?"

The bartender looked at Ellie carefully, pointed his wand at her, muttered his spell, but nothing happened.

He did the same thing to me, and it was so quick I didn't have the chance to protest at all. After all, I didn't know what this man's spell was doing, but I trusted him exactly zero percent.

"You're not law enforcement then," he said.

"Definitely not. I'm a baker, and this one's unemployed," she said, pointing her thumb towards me.

"In need of a little bit of luck then?" The man asked, and I nodded. "Fine. I'll take your bets. Who are your picks for tonight?"

"Miranda's Thunder," Ellie replied, handing over another envelope full of cash.

The bartender raised his eyebrows. "She's at 11 to 1 odds."

Ellie grinned. "I have a good feeling about her. Besides, I have to rep the thunder witches."

The man shrugged. "It's your money."

"We'll be back later. That shifter, did she tell you anything else about what she was doing here?"

The bartender considered Ellie for a minute before answering. "No."

"What did she bet on?"

"Duels, same as you. She wanted to know more than that, though. She asked what agency I was running through."

"And let me guess, you didn't exactly have registration papers to show her."

The man shrugged. "I'm just trying to make a living, like everybody else."

"So did she back off when she found out that you weren't running a strictly legal operation?"

"Nope. Still put her money here. She wanted to know who I reported to, but obviously I couldn't tell her that."

"Of course not."

Ellie got off her stool and I followed after her as we made our way back out into the blistering heat of the day.

"What was all that about?" I asked. "Was Chief Enforcer King here for gambling?"

Ellie shrugged. "She was, but I think it was part of her investigation. Paranormals are absolutely allowed to gamble, and there are plenty of registered places to do it legally. The underground places often offer better odds, since their overhead is lower and they don't need to pay the registration fees to the over-seeing committees. But the underground places are illegal."

"So would she be here on a case?" I asked. "After all, this isn't Western Woods."

"That's the thing," Ellie said with a bit of a frown. "There's no reason why Chief Enforcer King should be trying to solve a case here, since she has no jurisdiction here."

"And there wouldn't be any problem with her gambling here legally?"

"Not unless she was doing it excessively," Ellie replied. "Gambling doesn't really have negative connotations in the paranormal world. It's totally normal to put money on a duel."

"Yeah, speaking of, what are these duels? Who is Miranda Thunder?"

We don't have them in Western Woods, but duels involve a couple of witches or wizards going up against one another and using their spells to try and defeat the other person."

"So it's basically like magical boxing?"

"Yeah, exactly."

"Is it hard?"

"It depends who your opponent is," Ellie grinned. "The athletes who compete in duels have often been training for it for years and years. They're versed in all of their coven's spells of aggression and defense, and they often learn other covens' spells as well for maximum flexibility. On the other hand, because they've trained so specially for years and years, they often don't know a lot of basic spells most ordinary witches and wizards know."

"Why doesn't Amy do it? Being good at casting spells is definitely something that applies to her."

"For one thing, Amy hates the idea of duels. She doesn't think witches and wizards should fight each other, even for entertainment, and thinks there are more important spells to learn than fighting ones. And on top of that, duels take place in a lot of different towns. She would have to get up the courage to travel between towns regularly. She wouldn't do it to go to

Spellford, so she never would have done it for duels, either."

I nodded. That made a lot of sense. Amy wasn't really the adventurous type, either. While she was an incredible witch, she definitely didn't have the personality type to be an elite athlete, even if she had skills.

"Is Miranda Thunder any good?"

Ellie grinned at me. "On paper, not really. She hasn't won any fights in a while, and she isn't exactly the best out there, but she's a fighter. Miranda is one of the moons of Uranus, and they're also a Thunder coven. I've met her a couple of times and she's nice, which was why I put my money on her."

"I'm guessing you're not a regular gambler then," I said with a grin. "Betting money on somebody because they're nice doesn't seem like a winning strategy to me."

"You never know," Ellie said to me with a wink. "Besides, I know she's more than just nice. Tonight, she is going up against The Obelisk, from the coven of Oberon."

"So?"

"So while normally The Obelisk would be able to beat her relatively easily, I know for a fact that there has been a lot of tension between the coven of Miranda and the coven of Oberon lately. I don't know the details, but I know that a member of the coven of Oberon was accused of stealing a priceless heirloom from the coven of Miranda. So Miranda's Thunder –

ok, her real name is Fiona - definitely has a lot of reasons to want revenge tonight."

"And you're hoping that the extra incentive will make her a better fighter than she normally is, right?"

"At 11 to 1 odds, I'm absolutely willing to bet on that," Ellie said to me. Before we had a chance to continue, however, one of the golden chariots that had taken us into town from the pyramid suddenly stopped in front of us.

A moment later, the door opened, and Sara jumped out.

"Great. I was hoping I'd be able to find you guys."

## CHAPTER 13

"What are you doing here?" I asked as Sara closed the door behind her and the chariot slid off gracefully.

"It turned out I wasn't needed at work today, and when I came home, no one was around. My familiar told me where you guys had gone, and so I took the portal over here as well, hoping that I'd be able to find you and give you a hand."

"Great," Ellie said, catching Sara up on what we had discovered about Chief Enforcer King. "So now we know she was gambling, the only thing we don't know is why. It wouldn't have been just for fun, she would have gone somewhere with a license. None of this underground stuff."

Sara frowned slightly. "I have a cousin who lives here. I don't know her well; she's actually my second cousin, and she was born into this coven, but we are related. I actually forgot she lived here; I called my mom this morning while I was at work and told her what was going on, and she reminded me. We could go and see if she knows anything."

"We do have three hours before the duels start," Ellie said, looking at her phone. "Let's do it. Where does she work?"

Fifteen minutes later the three of us were sitting in a saloon style restaurant, where every single item on the menu was some variation of spaghetti. I had to admit, the Spaghetti Western theme was definitely growing on me. This was the restaurant where Sara's cousin had told us to meet her, and as soon as the girl slipped into the booth across from us, I knew she just had to be related to Sara.

Her hair wasn't quite as red; it had a bit of a brownish tinge to it, but I would have recognized those same green eyes anywhere. We could have been on the moon and I would know this girl was related to Sara. Boy, were those Leach genes powerful.

"Hey, Sara," the girl greeted Sara, before nodding at the rest of us.

"How's it going, Selena?" Sara replied with a smile. "It's been too long."

"It really has, hasn't it? But of course, it's so hard to get everyone together. I didn't know you were going to be in Desert Plains."

"Neither did I," Sara replied. "It was really a last minute thing, so thank you so much for meeting us."

"Anything for family," Selena answered as she picked up the menu. "As long as you buy me spaghetti, feel free to pick my brain as much as you want," she added with a wink.

"We were hoping you could help us with something the Chief Enforcer in our town might have been investigating here," I said. "We know that she placed a bet at one of the witch bars, but we don't know why. We don't think she was doing it for fun, we think it might have been part of an investigation."

"Which bar was it?"

"The Magic Brew," I replied, and I couldn't help but notice Selena's eyebrows rise. "So there is something strange about that place?"

"There have been rumors," Selena said. "I can't substantiate any of them, as I don't know the details and I don't work there, but I do work in gambling in this town. My day job is working for a registered gambling outfit, but I also answer the phones for a hotline at night for an organization that may not be quite as up-to-date on their license as they should be."

"Okay, so you have your nose to the ground when it comes to gambling, right?" Ellie interrupted, leaning forward enthusiastically.

Selena nodded. "Yeah. At least, I like to think I do."

"So what's going on at The Magic Brew?" Sara asked.

"Well, there have been rumors going around that they've gotten into more than just taking bets. Magic in gambling has always been difficult to deal with. After all, an errant witch could cast a spell during a duel to take down the opponent they don't want to win. It used to happen, as I'm sure you know. Now, of course, spells have been placed on the arena to stop that sort of thing, but there has still been the occasional crime ring that's tried to use magic to get an advantage when gambling. For the last couple of months, there has been a rumor that The Magic Brew has been taking their gambling proceeds and re-betting them, but not honestly. They're cheating to make money."

"But why would Chief Enforcer King be looking into that?" I asked. "That has nothing to do with Western Woods."

"It must somehow," Ellie frowned. "Because you're right, otherwise it wouldn't make any sense for her to be looking into it."

"Why are you guys looking into your chief inspector anyway?" Selena asked.

"She disappeared a couple of days ago," I replied. "No one has been able to find her, and we think there's a chance that her disappearance could be linked to the murder of one of our professors."

Selena's mouth dropped open. "Oh, that astronomy professor from your coven? We heard about that over here. An absolute tragedy."

"Did you know her at all?" I asked. After all, if

Professor Lei did have something to do with Desert Plains, it could lend credence to the idea that maybe chief inspector King's disappearance was linked to the professor's death.

Selena shook her head. "No, I never did. No one else I'd spoken to about it mentioned ever seeing her either."

Great. There went that theory. We paused for a minute while a waitress came by to take our orders; I got the spaghetti carbonara, since it had been a long time since I had had the dish.

"What do you know about this gambling thing at The Witch's Brew?" Ellie asked, getting the conversation back on track.

Selena shrugged. "Not much, really. I don't even know if there's anything to it. All I know is what I've heard from others. I don't know how it's done, but the group is taking money and placing large bets that end up working out for them, even when the odds say they shouldn't."

"Can you give us anything to work with?" Ellie asked.

Selena shrugged again. "As I said, there's nothing solid on this group out there. The only thing I know is the name of the person in charge. Aquila. And again, I have no idea how true that is. That's all I've got for you, sorry."

"Thanks," Sara said with a smile to her cousin. "That's helpful."

"I wish I could give you more, but I just haven't really heard anything else. The group is being very secretive. Of course, I can understand why. No one wants to go around advertising the fact that they're running some sort of gambling ring."

Just then, the waitress came by with plates laden full of huge servings of spaghetti, and the conversation was forgotten as the four of us dug in to our food. I hadn't realized just how hungry I was until the aroma of spaghetti mingled with egg and Parmesan cheese wafted to my nostrils.

"So do you guys think someone from Western Woods was involved in this gambling ring?" I asked through a giant mouthful after a few minutes.

"That seems likely, at least to me," Ellie replied. She was busy eating a meatball that had to be the size of her fist.

"I agree," Sara nodded. "If it was just a Desert Plains thing, then there would be no reason for Chief Enforcer King to get involved. That has to be it."

"For what it's worth, I can't say I've seen too many people from your neck of the woods hanging out here," Selena said. "If someone involved is from Western Woods, then they're being quite subtle about it."

Ellie nodded. "I would expect them to be; after all, you don't manage to run an allusive gambling ring without learning to hide pretty well."

As the four of us finished eating our spaghetti, the conversation moving on to other topics, I couldn't help but think that if even Chief Enforcer King couldn't bring this person to justice, what chance did the rest of us have?

## CHAPTER 14

*O*nce we finished eating, Selena thanked us, said goodbye to Sara - with the promise to stop by if she was ever in Western Woods - and Ellie, Sara, and myself all made our way towards the arena which was going to hold that night's witch's duel. After all, what better place to get insider information about gambling than a dueling tournament on which bets were placed?

I had no idea *how* we were going to get that information, but hey, what did we have to lose?

To my surprise, the dueling arena on the outskirts of town was a lot like a roman coliseum, but with a bit of a western touch. Instead of being built out of stone, the huge structure was made of wood, and all around the outside were magical portrayals of witches and wizards - I assumed the ones that were competing tonight - fighting each other as though projected onto the walls. By now, I knew a lot better than to look for an actual projector, these images were obviously put in magically.

Ellie, Sara, and I joined the queue of people making their way inside the stadium. Evidently, this was an incredibly popular pastime, and all-around people whopped and hollered while cheering and calling out the names of their preferred competitors. It definitely was not unlike the scene outside of CenturyLink Field when the Seahawks were playing.

While jerseys didn't seem to be much of a thing, a lot of the fans were specific colors, which I figured indicated that they were fans of certain competitors. A mustard yellow and black wearing woman had "Miranda Thunder" written on the back of her shirt, so I figured those must have been her colors.

A fairy fluttered past me a moment later, her royal blue shirt featuring a large, white oblong rock on the front of it. She obviously had to be cheering for Maranda's opponent tonight.

After about ten minutes of standing in line, the three of us made our way to the front, where we were briefly checked by security and let inside.

"We don't need tickets or anything?" I asked, and Ellie shook her head.

"No, the organization that runs the duels doesn't charge for entry; they make so much more money by licensing the rights to gamble that it's not worth it.

Besides, free entry means a packed stadium every night, which means good publicity."

I nodded as the three of us made our way to the main arena and found ourselves some seats. We were about halfway up, and as soon as we stepped out into the Stadium my head began to spin as I realized just how high up we were.

The floor of the arena had to be built down below ground level; we were at least three stories higher than the dusty arena floor. I grabbed at a railing and made my way down the steps with the others until we came across three empty seats, which we promptly took.

"I'll go get snacks, save my seat," Ellie said once we sat down, and made her way back from where we had just arrived.

"Have you ever seen one of these duels?" I asked Sara, and she shook her head.

"No, never. I see the results, of course. And I've watched them on TV. But I've never seen one live. To be honest, I'm not the biggest fan. Growing up we always played duels amongst ourselves, since that's what you do when you're little witches. But for me, it was never a fun experience, since everyone beat me all the time."

"I can understand that," I nodded. "Kids can be cruel."

"Especially Amy, since she had all of the talents that she still possesses with none of the humility that comes with being older than seven."

"Oooh, that would have sucked."

"She apologized for it all a few years ago. She told us that she didn't understand why any of us were even friends with her, given how she acted when we were little."

"What did you say to that?"

"I told her that I didn't know why I was friends with her, either," Sara replied with a laugh. "But I mean, that's what kids do. Obviously, I didn't hold a grudge."

I nodded as Ellie came back, carrying a tray laden full of food and drinks, and waving a brochure in her other hand.

"Sara, have a look at this," Ellie said, thrusting the piece of paper into Sara's hand.

I peeked over Sara's shoulder, curiosity piquing my interest, and read the brochure that Ellie had handed over.

*Wanted: Witches and Wizards with Skills on a Broom*

*Are you a witch or wizard with exceptional flying skills? Desert Plains Duels is currently searching for new talent to take part in a new sport that will rock the magical world: broom racing. Competitors will be required to fly with not only speed, but also skill as they avoid obstacles in a sport that will test their physical limits but also potentially bring glory that they have never envisioned. If this sounds like something you would be capable of doing, please send an audition video showcasing your broom riding skills to Desert Plains Duels by September 30th.*

I raised my eyebrows and looked at Sara. "That looks interesting."

"That's what I thought," Ellie said. "They had a bunch of these brochures out by the concession stand, and as soon as I saw it I thought of you, so I grabbed one."

"I don't know," Sara said slowly.

"What's not to know? You're easily the best witch in Western Woods on a broom," Ellie said.

"Maybe, but I doubt I stack up compared to others. What about all of the witches from the covens ruled by air? Surely, they're going to have a ton of witches and wizards who are a lot better than me."

"They might, but they might not," Ellie retorted. "You'll never know if you don't try out. Besides, this could be an amazing opportunity for you. Riding your broom has always been your favorite part of being a witch, and what if these broom races take off? You know how popular the best duelers are. Maybe that could be you. Speedy Sara. Striking as fast as a bolt of Jupiter's lightning."

Even Sara couldn't help but smile at that one. "Okay, fine. I'll look into it a little bit more."

"Good, I was hoping you would say that," I said. "I agree with Ellie. It could be really good for you. And you are really good at riding your broom."

Sara gave me a small smile of encouragement. "Thanks," she said, but I had a feeling that she wasn't completely sold on the idea just yet.

Ellie handed us small tubs of what looked like a multicolored popcorn, and I peered at it curiously. I wasn't especially hungry, seeing as I had just finished a giant plate of spaghetti a little while earlier, but this looked so strangely enticing, I kind of wanted to know what it was. And how it tasted.

"It's called pep pop," Ellie told me, noticing the strange expression on my face. "It's super low calorie, so I figured it would be appropriate given how much spaghetti we just ate. But it's magically enchanted to make you want to get up and cheer, so they sell it at all of these events to get the crowd going."

"The more I learn about magical food, the more I'm pretty sure this is what the human world would be like if all drugs were legal and everyone was taking them all the time," I joked. "What kind of drink is that?"

"Just water," Ellie said with a grin. "It's so warm and dry out here, you get dehydrated without even noticing it."

"Thanks, mom," I said with a smile as I happily grabbed a large cup of water from the tray. I took a careful bite of some of the pep pop, and immediately felt my mood rise, like I knew something cool was about to happen. Wow, these magical foods really did work quickly.

A few minutes later, just after the sun dipped over the horizon and the sky went from a deep blue to black, the lights in the Stadium came on and a hush came over the crowd.

"Witches, wizards, fairies, shifters, vampires, and more. Welcome, one and all to the most riveting fight in the paranormal world," an amplified voice boomed over the crowd. "Tonight, we have three duels with which to entertain you. First of all, The Titan takes on The Fires of Hell. Then, Fighting Luna takes on Thomas the Terrible."

"Well, Thomas the Tank Engine sure went badly somewhere along the lines," I muttered to myself.

"What's that?" Sara asked next to me.

"Nothing, just a human world joke," I replied.

"Finally, the fight you've all come here to see. Miranda Thunder takes on The Obelisk. But first, help me in welcoming our first two competitors: The Titan, and The Fires of Hell!"

The crowd erupted in a deafening roar, and I found myself jumping to my feet along with everyone else, despite the fact that I had no idea who either of the two competitors were. The pep pop was definitely doing its job after all.

"The Titan is actually not from the coven of Titan, but rather from the coven of Titania, which is a little bit confusing," Ellie said into my ear as the two men walked out from opposite ends of the Coliseum and into the arena. "He's the one dressed in blue and orange." Sure enough, the man on the far end, to our left, came out wearing blue and orange striped robes that gave him a real Harry Potter look. He looked small, but strong. "He's a young up and comer," Ellie continued. "Last year was his first season on the professional dueling circuit at the top level, and he managed to topple a couple of witches and wizards who were on paper much better than he is. He's a real wildcard, but he's cemented the fact that he deserves to be here."

"And the other guy?" I asked, looking over at The Fires of Hell, who didn't seem to be wearing anything at all, but was in fact engulfed in flames.

"The Fires of Hell. He's a legend on the circuit; he's been around for years and has won the dueling title for most wins at least eight times. He's from the coven of Charon, which I'm sure you can guess is ruled by fire."

I nodded as the amplified voice came over the crowd again.

"The competitors have entered the arena. Let the battle commence."

## CHAPTER 15

*I* let out a gasp as the night sky above us suddenly turned into an enormous Jumbotron. The wizards below looked tiny from where we sat, but the night sky made them look absolutely huge.

The Fires of Hell pulled out a wand, and muttered something that I couldn't make out. All I could see was his lips moving as I looked up to the giant display of the fight overhead. Suddenly, a large stream of fire emanated from his wand directly towards The Titan, who muttered a spell of his own and suddenly made the stream of fire turn into a tornado, a tornado which turned and began streaking back along the arena floor towards its creator.

My mouth dropped open and I watched as The Fires of Hell cast another spell and caused the tornado to duplicate itself, then triplicate itself, and continue multiplying. Within seconds there were at least fifteen, maybe twenty tornadoes moving along the arena floor.

The Titan moved swiftly around them, and when an errant flame caught at the base of his rope, a quick water spell extinguished the fire almost effortlessly. These guys definitely were good.

The Fires of Hell attacked again, obviously seeing that he was in the better position given as the flames didn't seem to be affecting him at all. He cast a spell and pointed his wand toward The Titan, but nothing happened.

The Titan darted around a fire tornado once more, then attacked himself. He muttered a spell, and suddenly The Fires of Hell began spiraling upwards, spinning like a top as his feet left the ground and moving faster and faster. The crowd roared as The Titan used his wand to fly The Fires of Hell around the arena before finally dropping him directly into the center of a fire tornado.

I let out a gasp of horror when suddenly, everything in the arena stopped. The fire tornados all dissipated, the projection of the show in the sky ended, and the crowd burst into cheers as the announcer's voice boomed once more.

"The winner of this duel: THE TITAN!" Looking down at the arena floor, The Titan raised his arms in triumph as The Fires of Hell lay on the ground, a swarm of Healers rushing towards him. A moment after they arrived he sat up; obviously whatever had happened didn't injure him permanently.

I joined in as the crowd celebrated the win, fans of the The Fires of Hell sitting dejectedly in their seats as everyone around them cheered.

As I looked around, however, I suddenly recognized one of the students who had been waiting for the same exam as Amy. It was one of Professor Lei's students. Why was she here? Was it a coincidence? Or could it have something to do with Chief Inspector King's disappearance and Professor Lei's murder? I decided that no matter what, I was going to find out.

I slipped past Ellie and back into the stairway, making my way down towards where I had seen the witch. I watched as her brown-hair had passed through a tunnel and back towards the concourse, and I slipped in after her. It wasn't too hard to follow the witch; I figured that between duels there was a little bit of a break, especially since it seemed like everybody in the stands was heading towards the concourse right now.

When we made it into the concourse, I began to try to catch up to the witch, and I chided myself for being silly. She was probably just coming out to get more food, or drink, or something. But instead, she walked straight past all of the concession stands and made her way towards the corner kind of isolated away from everyone else.

I half hid behind a beam, looking at the woman while pretending to be waiting for somebody.

Suddenly, I realized I could definitely have her identified quickly. Pulling out my phone, I pretended to be taking a panorama photo, but instead, I took a picture of the woman's face and immediately texted it to both Ellie and Sara, asking them who it was.

Sara was the first to answer: *That's Kelly Treach! Where are you?*

*In the concourse. I saw her, recognized her, and followed her.*

*What is she doing?*

*I don't know. Standing around.*

Just as I sent that last reply, however, Kelly began to do something. A man came out, seemingly out of nowhere. He was tall, dark, handsome, and 100% vampire. Every time he smiled he showed off his fangs, and he looked at Kelly like he wanted to sink his teeth deep into her.

The guy might have been good looking, but there was something incredibly creepy about him. I did not trust the guy at all.

I needed to figure out a way to get closer to the two of them, but I had no idea how. Unlike Ellie, I did not know how to cast an invisibility spell, and I certainly did not know anything more complicated like a sound amplification spell or anything like that. I began to kick myself for running off so quickly without telling the others where I was going, since now I was stuck here with my very limited magical skills, and no way to listen in to their conversation.

Kelly and the vampire were huddled close to one another, and it looked like they were having an argument. I really needed to know what was going on here.

Eventually, I made a decision. I texted Ellie. *What's the incantation to do an invisibility spell?*

*Are you going to try one?* Ellie replied a minute later.

*Yeah. It's important.*

*Jupiter with your power so mythical, turn this woman in front of me invisible. Then point the wand at yourself.*

*Thanks* I texted really quickly before pulling my wand out of my pocket, going to a quiet corner, and trying the spell.

I did everything Amy had been teaching me to do when casting spells. I emptied my mind, took a deep breath, and focused on the energy inside of me.

"Jupiter with your power so mythical, turn this woman in front of me invisible," I said, pointing at myself with the wand. When I opened my eyes, however, absolutely nothing had happened. The spell had failed.

I sighed, but tried to look on the bright side. After all, I hadn't accidentally turned myself into a toad or anything like that. There were worse things than a spell simply failing completely, as Sara could attest to.

Pushing the failure into the back of my head, I took another deep breath, and tried once more. Again, nothing.

This time, I was starting to feel a little bit more

dejected. I felt like I was doing everything right, so why wasn't it working?

After my third failed attempt, I finally pulled out my phone and texted Ellie.

*It's not working.*

*Oh, I forgot, it won't work while you're in this building. It's one of the ways they prevent cheating; there's a powerful ward on the entire arena to prevent magic from being used.*

Well, at least the reason that spell hadn't worked wasn't that I was terrible at magic. But I'd wasted another thirty seconds trying to cast that spell, and I figured it was now or never. I had no other options now.

I tried to subtly slide towards Kelly and the vampire, pretending to text away on my phone and then stopping a few feet away from them, facing the vampire. After all, there was a better chance that Kelly would recognize me as being someone from Western Woods than him. To the vampire, I would just look like one of any of the thousands of other witches watching the duels tonight.

As I inched closer and closer, I strained my ears to listen. Luckily, years of working at a bar meant that I was able to pretty accurately drown out any ambient noise when I wanted to listen in to a conversation.

"You're short a thousand," the vampire hissed at Kelly.

"I know. Look, I know. I'll get it to you by the end of the week, ok?"

"That's what you said the last time."

"And you know what I did to work it off. I can't believe I did that."

"Yeah, well, when you owe Aquila abras, if you can't pay them, you have to work them off."

"I don't know if I can do it anymore. I can't believe I actually did that for her. You know I threw up after?"

"Whatever, I don't care about your emotions. I care about your cash. If you didn't want to work off your debt, maybe you shouldn't have bet more than you could pay."

"I know. Look, I know. I'm still behind. But please. Give me another couple of days."

"Fine. You have forty eight hours. Or I go back to Aquila, and she'll give you another job to do. And remember, there's no Chief Enforcer for you to go running to. You know what we can do to people: you tell anyone about this, and you'll disappear, too."

I tried not to react as I heard those words, but it was tough. It sounded like Kelly had been forced to do something she hadn't enjoyed. Something bad. Had she been forced to kill Professor Lei? Maybe we had the right suspect, but the wrong reason. It certainly sounded like she was in deep with these debt collectors, anyway.

And there was that name again – Aquila. It sounded like the rumors Selena had heard were real. Aquila was a real person, and he was in charge of this gambling ring that Kelly had somehow gotten herself involved in.

"I'll pay you," Kelly hissed to the vampire. "I promise. I'll pay you in just a couple of days."

"You had better," the vampire replied. "Meet me here again on Saturday night, same time, and this time you had better have all of it. Plus two hundred, for my time."

He turned and strode off, and I dared to glance at Kelly. The expression on her face screamed glumness and depression. I couldn't help but feel a little bit sorry for her. She didn't sound like she was the best person, but gambling addictions were an addiction, and this couldn't have been easy for her. Especially since she was being made to do things she didn't want to do. I wondered if that list of things included murder.

## CHAPTER 16

The announcer's voice boomed over the loudspeaker just then, inviting the audience to return to their seats ahead of the second duel. Instead of making my way back to the seat, however, I stepped towards Kelly.

"Hey," I said to her softly. "Are you alright?"

She looked up at me with a look of suspicion at first, but as soon as she saw who it was, her expression softened.

"Oh. You're from Western Woods. You're that new witch in town, right?"

I nodded. "Tina."

"I'm Kelly. Nice to meet you."

"You too. Listen, are you in some sort of trouble? That vampire looked like bad news?"

"Did you hear any of that?" she asked, fear written all over her face.

"No," I lied. "I was just coming out to find a restroom when I saw you talking to him, and you looked like you would have rather been anywhere else."

A small smile crept on Kelly's face. "Well, you've got that right. No, don't worry about me. I'm fine."

"Ok," I nodded, not wanting to push her. I didn't want her to know that I'd overheard a ton of that conversation. "Well, if you ever need anything, I'm around."

"Thanks," Kelly said, and as I made my way back to my seat, I couldn't help but feel a bit sad for Kelly. I knew the others didn't really think much of her, but it must have been difficult for her trying to hide an addiction like gambling and still try to live a normal life.

I really hoped the addiction hadn't forced her into something awful, like murder.

By the time I made my way back to my seat – I got lost once along the way, it turned out the colosseum was much larger than I had initially thought – Ellie and Sara looked over at me.

"You missed the second fight," Sara said. "It just ended. "Thomas the Terrible just *destroyed* Fighting Luna."

"Yeah, well, I just got some information that's way more interesting than that," I said, motioning for Sara and Ellie to come in closer. I didn't want anyone over-hearing what I was about to tell them.

"Wow," Sara said, shaking her head when I finished

recounting my story. "It sounds like Kelly's in deep, and she definitely had to do something bad to pay Aquila or whoever."

"Agreed," I said. "Plus, it gives credence to this Aquila actually existing. It sounds like Kelly owes him, big time."

"Do you think she might have been forced to kill Professor Lei, for some reason?" Ellie asked.

"I thought about that, but what could the Professor possibly have had to do with a gambling ring. Besides, at one point, the vampire said 'as you know, Chief Enforcer King isn't around' or something along those lines. What if they forced Kelly to do something to Chief Enforcer King?"

"Would she have been able to?" Sara asked. "After all, Chief Enforcer King can handle herself pretty well."

"She can, but against a witch? Even one who's not super skilled like Kelly? It's possible. After all, shifters can't cast spells. They have their own magic, but witches are inherently at an advantage against them."

"Maybe that's what it was then," I mused. "Maybe Kelly did something to Chief Enforcer King as payment for some of her debt."

"That would be truly awful," Ellie said, shaking her head sadly. "I really hope it's not something like that."

"Well, whatever it is, it doesn't sound like it was a good thing," Sara said.

Before we got a chance to discuss things further, however, the third fight was about to get underway.

"All right paranormals of the world, it's the moment you've all been waiting for. Please give a warm welcome to our last two competitors of the night, Miranda Thunder and The Obelisk. The crowd roared with appreciation as the arena floor was covered in a dense fog. More magic, I supposed. A few seconds later, the fog dissipated, and we found ourselves staring at the two competitors.

Miranda Thunder, on the far side, was small. She couldn't have been much taller than 5 feet, and she was slender. She moved with a confidence and an agility that made me think that she might've had some sort of gymnastics training. I had a friend growing up who did gymnastics, and Miranda absolutely reminded me of her. Her long, brown hair reached almost down to her waist, and she had an almost ethereal quality to her. If you had told me that she was half witch, half fairy, I would have believed you.

The Obelisk, on the other hand, fit his chosen dueling name perfectly. He had to be at least six feet tall, and well and truly powered over Miranda. His pudgy belly and small head gave him a real Obelisk-like look, like a large chunk of rounded rock.

The two competitors stared each other down, and as the announcer declared that the fight had started, both of them immediately attacked.

I found myself riveted as they each cast spell after spell. When one would attack, the other would cast a defensive spell, resulting in a stalemate. Both were obviously extremely talented fighters. Miranda kept calling down thunder and lightning, and the deafening sound of the thunder roared through the arena.

The Obelisk attempted to bring down some rocks to crush Miranda, but she managed to use lightning as a defensive shield, and cracked all of the boulders until they were no more than pebbles falling at her feet. Casting a spell, all of the pebbles rose up and darted back towards The Obelisk at a lightning speed. He raised his wand to cast a defending spell, but just as he cast it the pebbles rushing towards him split into two groups, one going to the left and one going to the right, before doubling back and attacking him from the side.

He let out a yelp as Miranda's spell hit him right on. Throwing up his wand into the air, a fury of white sparks emanated from it, and a moment later all of the pebbles, along with all other signs of the duel, disappeared.

"The white sparks in the air means he gave up," Ellie explained to me. "As soon as the fight is declared over, all the spells are automatically dissolved, so as to lower the risk of injury to the athletes."

I nodded my understanding as realization dawned on me. "I guess we need to go back to that bar to collect your winnings."

Ellie grinned at me. "I told you I knew what I was doing."

She certainly did.

CHAPTER 17

The three of us made our way back to The Witch's Brew to collect on Ellie's eleven to one win. I couldn't help but wonder what was going to happen. After all, this was apparently the gambling ring's headquarters. And Ellie wasn't exactly known for being shy.

The three of us walked in, and Sara and I followed as Ellie immediately made her way towards the bartender.

"Here for your winnings?" the bartender asked. "I'm not sure I should give them to you. How do I know you didn't have some sort of inside info? After all, I've never seen you before, and here you come betting on some unlikely winner and you come out making ten times your money. You can't blame me for being suspicious."

"Why don't we ask Aquila what he thinks?" Ellie

said, leaning across the bar towards the bartender. He immediately looked around, checking to make sure that nobody had overheard.

"You keep your voice down," he hissed at her. "Ain't nobody here named Aquila."

"Where can I find him?" Ellie asked. "You tell me that, and you can keep the money."

"Wouldn't be worth any amount of money to give you that information," the bartender replied. "Besides, even if I wanted to help you, I couldn't. Never laid eyes on the man myself."

"I'll take my money then," Ellie said. "You can think what you want about me, but if you don't pay me what I'm owed I'll make sure the authorities know about this illegal gambling ring you're running."

The bartender grumbled and handed over an envelope. It was thick with cash; Ellie had definitely made out extremely well from her betting today.

"Look. I can't help you, and you didn't hear this from me, but there is a vampire in town who might know the information you're after. You can find him at Caesar's Palace, a vampire bar in town. He's there every night. He won't like you showing up to visit him, though."

Ellie slid a few bills across the table at the bartender, nodded at him, and the three of us left the bar. It looked like we knew where our next stop was.

"Do you have any idea where that bar is?" I asked. Caesar's Palace was a hilarious name for a bar in a town that was so similar, and yet in other ways so different to Las Vegas.

"No idea," Ellie said. "Luckily, in this place, you don't need to know where something is to get to it."

As if on cue, one of the floating golden chariots arrived and stopped right in front of us. Ellie motioned for Sara and me to get in first, and we did so, a warm glow of light filling the interior of the chariot now that the sun had gone down.

Ellie got in after us, and as soon as she closed the door behind her, the chariot floated off, stopping a few minutes later in front of a building that I initially thought had been abandoned. The windows were all boarded up, and no light seeped through. However, a moment later, two female vampires left via the front door and as soon as it opened the sound of pounding music reached my ears. Evidently, even though it looked deserted from out here, there was still something going on in there.

I raised my eyebrows at the others and passed through the door, with Ellie and Sara following after me. We found ourselves in a tiny room, with a large sign that read 'Please allow the outside door to close fully behind you before entering in order to minimize light leakage'. I did as the sign asked, waiting a couple of moments for Ellie and Sara to get in as well and for the door to close behind us, before I pushed in through the second door and entered the vampire bar at Caesar's Palace.

I let my eyes adjust to the low light, a couple of candles placed here and there being the only emitters. I was tempted to take out my phone and turn on the flashlight to get a better look at the patrons, but I had a sneaking suspicion that wouldn't exactly be appreciated by the clientele here. If I had learned one thing about vampire bars, it was that the patrons definitely did not appreciate extra sources of light while they were drinking.

"How are we going to know who we're after?" Sara whispered.

"There," I said, pointing to the vampire I had seen speaking with Kelly. As soon as the bartender had told us there was a vampire involved, I was almost certain it was him that he was talking about. Sure enough, he was here now.

The three of us made our way over to the table where the vampire was drinking something unidentifiable - he was pretty far from the nearest candle - and as the three of us sat across from him, his expression didn't change at all.

"This is not a bar for witches."

"Do you want to talk elsewhere?" Ellie said.

"I don't want to talk."

"Well, that's too bad, because I have all this money here and I guess maybe I'll go spend it with someone who does want to talk."

Ellie pulled out a stack of bills, and the vampire practically drooled as he looked at the money.

"All right, what is it you want to know?"

"Start with the basics. What's your name?"

"Anton."

"All right, Anton. I hear you're neck-deep in Aquila's gambling ring."

"I don't know what you're talking about."

"Right. Of course you don't."

"I heard you talking to Kelly today in the concourse at the arena," I said, and Anton looked at me carefully. I did not like the look he was giving me at all.

"Fine. But if anyone else asks about it, I'll deny I told you anything."

"That works for us," Ellie said. "As far as we're concerned, as soon as we leave this building, this conversation never happened."

Anton nodded, and Ellie took a seat at the table across from him. Sara and I followed her cue and did the same.

"Where do we go to find Aquila?"

Anton laughed, a dry, mean laugh with no humor behind it. "Yeah, right. You're never going to see him. Even I don't know who Aquila is."

"We were told you could get to him."

Anton shook his head. "Aquila as a ghost. I've spoken to him on the phone, and I've organized drop-offs, and I've even stayed behind to see if I could catch a glimpse of him, but it never happens."

"Do you know what kind of paranormal he is?" I asked.

"He has to be a wizard. Only a wizard would be able to create the magic required to hide himself from me when he collects the money that I drop off for him."

"What does his voice sound like?" Sara asked.

"Changed. It's definitely not a natural human voice. To be honest, I can't even say for sure Aquila is a he."

"Do you know if he was involved in Chief Enforcer King's disappearance, the Chief Enforcer from Western Woods?" Ellie asked.

"Wouldn't be worth my life to tell you that," Anton said, shaking his head. "I've already told you too much. This conversation is over."

He turned away and Ellie shrugged at us, and the three of us turning and leaving the bar. That hadn't been nearly as productive as I had hoped it would be.

With nothing left to do in Desert Plains, the three of us took the chariot back to the portal and made our way back to Western Woods.

As soon as we got home, the three of us flopped down in the living room while Amy came out with a bottle of wine. She popped the bottle and handed out glasses. "Going by the look of the three of you, you could definitely use these," she said.

"Yeah, what idiot had the idea of getting us water instead of alcohol to watch the duel?" I teased with a smile, and Ellie stuck her tongue out at me.

"I'm guessing you didn't get to interview Kelly Treach?" I said to Amy as she poured out a glass of wine.

"That's right, how did you know?"

"We saw her, in Desert Plains," I replied, and the three of us spent the next twenty minutes taking turns telling Amy everything that had happened that day.

When we finished, Amy let out a low whistle. Wow, and I thought *my* day was interesting."

"What did you find out?" I asked.

"Well, for one thing, Professor Lei was probably having an affair. That would be a pretty good reason for the fight she had with her husband a few days before she was murdered."

"Not to mention, a pretty good motive for murder. Do you know who the affair was with?"

Amy leaned in and answered in a hushed voice, even though we were the only people in the house right now. "I think it might have been Professor Fulgur."

"Who?" I asked.

"John Fulgur, you met him the other day," Ellie told me.

"Oh, right. Him. Oh," I said again, my eyes widening. "Really?"

"That's the rumor," Amy said. "I don't know if it's true. But Professor Thor was telling me that they've been seen together a lot, and there have been whispers about them being more than just colleagues."

"Well, that can just be idle chatter as well," Sara said. "After all, they might just be good friends."

Amy smiled. "That's what I thought, too. So I snuck a truth serum into a Hexpresso Bean coffee that I brought over to him. He didn't suspect a thing. That's one advantage to being one of the most trustworthy witches in the coven. I felt really bad about it, and I wasn't going to do it, but then I realized that if there was a chance he was the murderer, then didn't I owe it to Professor Lei to find out?"

"Oh, that's so smart," Ellie said.

"Wait," I said. "Didn't you tell me once that truth serums don't allow you to get answers to questions that might get someone in major trouble? That's why we can't use them to rule out murderers?"

"That's right," Amy nodded. "So I had to be careful about what questions I asked. I started off by asking if he was spending more time with Professor Lei than he did a few years ago. His answer to that that yes, he was. I asked if that time they spent together was outside of a professional setting, and he confirmed that yes, it was."

"So they almost certainly were having an affair," Ellie said with a slow nod.

"It appears that way," Amy said. "I did ask him if he and Professor Lei shared any hobbies outside of work; if they were both members of the same book club, for example, that would rule out an affair but also give me an affirmative answer to his other questions. He said that no, they didn't do any hobbies together."

"Were you able to confirm whether or not they were still together?" I asked.

"That came next, and it was a little bit harder to get out of him. Eventually, I asked Professor Fulgur if he and Professor Lei had spoken in the days leading up to her murder."

"And?" Ellie asked.

"He said they did, but he wasn't very forthcoming, which I thought was suspicious. So I asked if they had an argument, and he wouldn't answer, which meant I was treading in too dangerous waters for the truth serum. So I asked instead if Professor Lei started an argument with him, and he said she had. I asked if Professor Lei had said she didn't want to see him again, and he said yes."

"So she broke up with him," Ellie said slowly. "That's a pretty good motive for murder right there."

"That's what I thought," Amy said. "What if the argument came from Professor Lei's husband finding out the affair? And then she decided she wanted to end it with Professor Fulgur, and he didn't like being dropped like that?"

"That would be a pretty good motive for murder," I agreed.

"I think we need to find out whatever we can about this Aquila person, though," Ellie said. "I think he – or she – is the key to the whole thing. Even if it's nothing to do with Professor Lei's murder, I think it's got something to do with Chief Enforcer King's disappearance, and I want to investigate it further."

"How are we going to manage that, though?" I asked. "After all, I think Anton was probably the closest we're going to have come to meeting Aquila, and he said that he has never met Aquila, either."

"Who knows?" Ellie said. "We can cross that bridge when we get to it. Tomorrow is Professor Lei's funeral, though, so why don't we make that our next step? We'll go there, and we'll see what we can discover. I think as far as this whole Aquila thing goes, we figured out as much as we can for now. But tomorrow, at the funeral, we can investigate Kelly, as well as Professor Lei's husband, and her probably former lover John."

"Good plan," Sara said, and I nodded. Slowly but surely, we were going to get to the bottom of this murder, even if we didn't quite know which avenue to follow just yet.

## CHAPTER 18

The next morning, I watched as my three roommates all dressed in long, flowing robes. They were a dark green, with a silver effect that gave the impression of lightning strikes every time they took a step.

"You can borrow one of my formal robes," Ellie said. "We could have bought you a set when we went to get you clothes from Randy's store when you first got here, but to be honest, we didn't think that you were going to end up going to a witch funeral so quickly."

"I'd be a lot happier if I hadn't," I said with a smile. "That's not real lightning on the robes, is it?"

Ellie grinned at me. "No, of course not. It's just a magical effect to give that impression. Every coven has their own set of formal robes, and obviously ours is lightning based."

"Right," I nodded. "So it's okay for me to wear one of your robes?"

"Well, normally a witch is not allowed to wear the robes of another coven. However, since your situation is a little bit unique, and you don't know which coven you do belong to, it's more important for you to be dressed as a witch than it is for you to be dressed in the clothing of your specific coven. Once we discover which coven you belong to though, we will make sure you get a set of robes from that coven. For now, your adoptive coven is fine."

"Thanks," I said gratefully to Ellie. It was really nice of the coven of Jupiter to make me feel like I belonged, even though we didn't know which coven I was truly born into.

A few minutes later, I draped her robe over myself, and sure enough, even though every time I took a step my robe flashed with magical lightning, I couldn't feel anything. It was definitely pretty cool.

Twenty minutes later, the four of us made our way down to the lake, which was a part of coven gardens, and was where all witch and wizard funerals took place. All around were witches and wizards, all dressed in the same deep green robes with silver lightning flashing across every time they moved. From time to time, I saw someone wearing a different type of robe. There was a wizard obviously from a fire coven, whose robe was pure black, but every time he took a step, flames leapt up from the bottom of the robe. The faster his steps, the more intense the flame. Another witch, presumably from an Earth coven, wore a robe that seemed to camouflage her perfectly in the gardens. Sure enough, what Ellie had told me was obviously right: every coven had their own formal robes. It was quite interesting to see.

While the majority of the people attending were witches and wizards, given as the victim in our murder case was a witch, a number of the town's other residents also milled around here and there. I recognized a few of the fairies that worked at Hexpresso Bean, all huddled together, and a few shifters, including Orson Brown, milled around towards the back. I imagined they must've been there more for the investigative aspect than for grieving purposes.

While I had seen a funeral take place since moving to Western Woods, it had not been for a member of the coven of Jupiter, but for a member of the fire coven who lived here. I was a little bit curious as to what was going to happen. We arrived just in time, and before we had a chance to interact with anybody, a tall wizard that I recognized as the high priest for the coven of Jupiter made his way to the front of the chairs set up, raising his hands for silence.

As soon as the man raised his hands, everyone stopped talking and those who were still standing made their way towards the seats.

"Thank you all for coming to the funeral of Mai Lei, a stalwart in our coven's community. Mai worked as a professor, and her love of learning professed itself in everything she did. She studied the stars, and she studied numbers. The subjects some of us found the most difficult, she embraced with a tenacity and a determination matched by none. Mai also loved her husband and her children. They were everything to her. I had never thought that Mai Lei would ever find anything that would interest her more than the secrets of the night sky, but love has a of taking over people's lives in a way we can never imagine. Ever since Mai met Andrew, her heart was given over to him completely. And when they had the girls, I never saw a woman so determined to be such a good mother.

"Now, if all of you could please join me in singing the song of Jupiter as we release Mai's body back into the skies from which we came."

I had no idea what to expect next, but in the center of the lake, an island suddenly formed out of nowhere. It rose up like a submarine, water pouring off it from either side and causing large waves to lap at the side of the lake. In the center of the island was a large, black ball. It had to be at least twelve feet across.

As the island rose up, the sky above suddenly went dark. Black clouds covered the sky as far as the eye could see, and the rolling sound of thunder loomed overhead. A few cracks of electricity sparked in the sky, and I looked up in wonder.

The high priest opened his arms and looked up.

"Jupiter, God of the skies. Please, take the body of Mai Lei back to your home, to the land of thunder."

The sky above the large ball suddenly began to spin; kind of like what I imagined the eye of a hurricane would look like. A small hole opened up and cast down a ray of light directly onto the large black ball, and the priest began to chant.

It was a low, deep chant, kind of like the Gregorian chants that I had learned in school. Most of the crowd - all of the witches and wizards - joined in a moment later, and as the sound rose, so did the black ball. It left the magical island and floated straight up into the sky, directly into the hole in the clouds that had been formed. As soon as it crossed the threshold into the clouds, the clouds closed up and a storm of thunder and lightning, but no rain, poured down from the sky.

I had to admit, it was incredibly enchanting.

"Jupiter has taken back Mai Lei," the high priest announced. "Please, remember her time on earth amongst yourselves fondly."

With that, everyone began to get up from their chairs. I supposed that meant this part of the funeral was over. The four of us made our way to the tables nearby that were laden with food and drink, and I spotted Kyran out by the trees.

"I'll be back," I said to the others as I made my way towards him.

As soon as he saw me, however, Kyran turned and began to leave.

"Wait," I called out to him. "Hold up, I want to talk to you."

"Haven't I told you how bad of an idea this is?" Kyran asked. "Your life as a new witch here in Western Woods is going to be difficult as it is. You don't want to make it worse by being friends with me."

"Why don't you let me decide that for myself?" I asked, putting my hands on my hips.

"Because you don't know what you're getting into. I'm a pariah here, and it was stupid of me to think that I could possibly be your friend without it having negative consequences that would affect you."

"Well, people can think what they want. Negative consequences or not, I think you're okay, and what's the point of living if fear stops you from doing what you want?"

Kyran grinned. "I knew I liked you for a reason. Fine. If you insist on being associated with my pariah butt, then it's on you. But let me tell you now: if you ever decide that it's too much of a risk to be associated with me, I won't be offended."

"Got it," I said. "But don't worry, that's not going to happen. People in this town can dislike me for whatever reasons they want, but I've gotten in trouble over more things than who I associate with in Western Woods."

"Yeah, I guess getting almost murdered by people trying to hide the fact that they're killers will do that,"

Kyran said. "Speaking of, how close are you to finding Professor Lei's killer?"

I shrugged. "We have a whole bunch of leads, but nothing solid yet. We don't know if her murder is linked to the gambling ring in Desert Plains that Chief Enforcer King was investigating."

Kyran raised an eyebrow. "Aquila's gang?"

"How on earth do you know about that?" It seemed like any time I needed to know anything about the magical world, Kyran had the answer.

He smiled. "I make it my business to know what kind of unsavory activities are happening in this world. After all, it leaks into crime in the human world a lot more than you might think."

"Do you know who Aquila is?" I asked.

Kyran shook his head. "No, I didn't even know it was someone from Western Woods. It has to be, otherwise why would Chief Enforcer King be investigating it?"

"No one seems to know who Aquila is," I said, the frustration evident in my voice. "I'm sure whoever it is, they are linked to Chief Enforcer King."

"Maybe you need to look at things from a different angle," Kyran said. "If no one knows who Aquila is, figure out what the link is between Professor Lei and Chief Enforcer King. That link might be the key to solving the identity."

"Do you know more than you're telling me?" I asked, narrowing my eyes at Kyran.

He shook his head. "No, I'm just giving you general advice. While I know about Aquila's gang, it's not currently a priority for me and I don't have the time to try and figure out who Aquila is right now."

"Okay, thanks," I said. I looked back towards the tables where everyone was eating, and realized that this was actually a great opportunity to look for information while coven headquarters would be basically abandoned.

"You're thinking of going back into town?" Kyran said, and I sighed as I remembered that elves had this uncanny ability to not read exact thoughts, but definitely to be able to sense what a person was thinking.

"That ability is super creepy, you know?"

"Well, I think it's super creepy when you cast spells, so we're even."

"Fair enough."

"You've probably got about an hour before the witches start making their way back into town and coven headquarters is manned once more," Kyran told me. "I have to go. Stay out of trouble."

He gave me a little half bow, then turned and headed back towards Western Woods. I pulled out my phone and texted Sara, Amy, and Ellie. This was our chance.

## CHAPTER 19

Sure enough, Kyran had been right. When we got to coven headquarters, there was absolutely nobody there. It was completely deserted. There were a couple of wards on the doors set to stop unwanted intruders, but Amy made quick work of those and we found ourselves in Professor Lei's classroom, with no one else around, and the ability to finally look through her things to see if we could find a hint as to who murdered her.

I was specifically looking for anything that might have linked Professor Lei to Chief Enforcer King's investigation. After all, maybe Kyran was right. Maybe trying to uncover Aquila's identity was the wrong way to go. It hadn't really gotten us very far so far, but coming at the problem a different way might have been the key.

Ellie began going through some cabinets at the

back, while I sat down at Professor Lei's desk and found a large binder full of classroom summaries. Maybe the answer lay in something she was teaching?

"Hey Amy, tell me about the class you are taking with Professor Lei. But don't use your super smart words, tell me about it in a way that I would understand."

"It's about the mathematical theory used in astronomy," Amy explained. "Basically, we use math to calculate the trajectory of various celestial objects and how they impact one another."

"Wow, that was surprisingly dumbed down," Ellie said with a smile. "Normally, when you ask Amy a question, even when she factors in the fact that we are mere mortals who don't understand half of what she's talking about, it's still incomprehensible."

"Maybe the math stuff is the link between Professor Lei and Chief Enforcer King," I mused. "After all, gambling is basically math, right?"

"Well, as far as I know, cheating at gambling is," Ellie said. "In the human world, don't you have games like poker where people have a tendency to count cards to try and beat the odds?"

"Sure," I replied. "I imagine a lot of gambling in the magical world is the same?"

"Yeah."

"But, the problem is, Professor Lei's math skills weren't necessarily the sort of thing that would be used in a practical sense," Amy argued. "She was very much a theoretical mathematician, and most of the math we did in her classes related to astrology."

I flipped through the binder containing all of her coursework, and had to admit, it did look fairly complicated.

*Navigation on earth by following the stars.*

*Constellation name origins.*

*Orbits of moons in relations to their planets.*

*Predicting the death of stars based on mass and growth rate.*

Even the names of Professor Lei's lessons seemed complicated. And I had to admit, Amy was right: there was nothing here that would have indicated that Professor Lei did any sort of math that might relate to gambling. It was definitely all astronomy-based.

I let out a sigh after about twenty minutes. This was really going nowhere.

"Hey, Sara, have you thought some more about whether or not you're going to try out for that new broom flying competition?" Ellie asked, and Amy perked up.

"What broom flying competition?"

"I found a brochure for it when we were at the duels the other day. The company that runs the professional duels is starting a new sport, which involves broom flying. But Sara doesn't seem to be as enthusiastic about it as I thought she would be."

"Oh, that sounds interesting," Amy replied.

"I know! That's what I thought, too," Ellie said.

"I'm interested," Sara said. "I'm just trying not to get my hopes up."

"Hey, I'm going to go have a look around the rest of coven headquarters, ok?" I said. I wasn't sure I could add much to the current conversation, and I felt like maybe a little bit of a walk to clear my head would be a good idea.

"Sure," Amy nodded. "Just make sure you're out of the building in forty minutes, since the spells I've used to make sure our presence can't be detected will have worn off.

"Will do," I replied, leaving the three of them to keep looking around the office. I made my way out into the hall and sighed. I didn't know why, but I was suddenly overcome by a feeling of being overwhelmed, like no matter what I did I was never going to solve this case. It felt like no matter what angle I came at it from, it was never enough. I wasn't getting any closer to the answer.

Making my way down the hall, towards all of the other classrooms, I looked at the pictures on the wall. There were some of former coven leaders, some paintings of Jupiter, and a number of others as well.

I didn't really look at them too hard, or read the descriptions with any great detail, but I stopped suddenly when a single word underneath one of the paintings caught my eye.

It was a picture of a constellation, in sort of a T-shape. Underneath the picture, was the explanation.

*Aquila is a constellation on the celestial equator which represents the eagles which carried Jupiter's thunder in coven mythology.*

Aquila. That couldn't be a coincidence. There was absolutely no way. I stared at the picture, thinking hard about things. Aquila was the name taken by the leader of the gambling ring in Desert Plains. Chief Enforcer King's disappearance was right around the same time as Professor Lei's death. The professor had known a lot about both astronomy and math. Even if her math was more theoretical and didn't deal directly with gambling, what if we had it all wrong? What if Professor Lei was Aquila? After all, it sounded like no one knew who Aquila really was. It was possible that if Aquila had died, a few days would pass without anybody noticing anything had gone wrong down in Desert Plains.

I let out a long breath. This was definitely not what I had expected to find out when I considered looking at things from a different angle. And yet, it all made sense. Aquila may very well have been Professor Lei.

## CHAPTER 20

*M*aking my way back to the others, I immediately explained my theory. Amy shook her head slowly.

"It doesn't make any sense. I've known Professor Lei for years, and she's never seemed to me to be the type that would do something like this."

"You think that about all of our teachers, though," Ellie said.

"That's because it's true," Amy said, crossing her arms. "I've spent so much time with Professor Lei in this room, I can't imagine that she was running a gambling ring."

"There's an easy way to find out," I said. "Why don't we go back to Desert Plains, and ask Anton when he left the money to be picked up for Aquila? If it turns out that the money was being left while she had a class or something, then it's easily solved. We will know that it couldn't have been her. Seeing how secretive Aquila is about his or her identity, I can't imagine that they would have sent someone else to pick up the money and then have it delivered to them; I'd imagine they picked it up themselves."

Sara nodded. "That makes sense, I can definitely see that."

"Fine," Amy said. "Let's do it. I want to clear Professor Lei's name as soon as possible. She was a good professor, and if she was involved in this, I'm certain it was to help Chief Enforcer King, and that she was not the target of the investigation."

"Now?" Sara asked. I looked outside at the sun beginning to make its way towards the horizon. Sunset was maybe two hours away.

"Why not?" I asked. "After all, it's not going to be too long before the sun sets and the vampire bar opens. That's where we're going to find Anton."

~

The four of us made our way to the portal and quickly found ourselves transplanted on top of the Desert Plains pyramid. We climbed the steps down to ground level, but instead of grabbing a chariot, Amy pulled us aside.

"Why don't we walk to town, and on the way there, I can give Tina a lesson on desert plants? Ellie, you can help, since I know you know the plants very well also."

"Good idea," Sara said. "I'm always happy to tag along when Tina gets a lesson in the hopes of being able to pick something up myself."

With that settled, the four of us began to walk along a desert road, and I couldn't help but notice as I walked along that there really wasn't all that much here in terms of flora. A few succulents dotted the desert here and there, but that was about it.

"All right," Amy said, tearing off the path and towards a small clump of cacti. "The first thing you need to know about succulents is that even though they look like nothing, they almost all have magical properties."

"Kind of like how the aloe plant is good for sunburns?" I asked.

Ellie nodded. "Exactly like that, but in the magical world, you'll find that most of the succulents have more uses than just those. In fact, while it can be difficult to find certain plants in the desert, they can actually be life-saving. Like this one here."

Ellie reached down to show me a small plant with thick, greenish-blue leaves. "This is a blue star. As far as I know, in the human world, it's decorative only. However, the species that grows here can help with heart problems. If you ever find yourself running into somebody who's having a heart attack, feed them one of the leaves from this plant."

"Okay," I nodded, making sure to remember what the plant looked like.

"They use it at the hospital all the time," Sara added. "I know this one too." She pointed to a succulent next to the blue star that was similar in color – perhaps more turquoise than the blue star - but whose leaves were different. It almost looked like a whole bunch of small bananas were growing out of it. "This is an elegans blue. If you're ever bleeding profusely, chew up its leaves into a mash, and place it on the wound. It will stop the bleeding almost instantaneously."

"Okay," I nodded, getting a good look at that plant as well.

"One of the most important things to remember when it comes to desert plants is that the flowers of all of them have the same healing properties," Ellie said. "The flesh is different for each plant, but flowers from any desert plant that are ingested will cure stomach ailments."

"So like, nausea?" I asked.

"Exactly," Amy nodded. "Also heartburn, ulcers, and anything else that can affect the stomach. To a lesser extent, they can help with intestinal issues as well, but because most of the healing properties have left the flower by the time they reach the intestine, it's not as powerful as using them for stomach ailments."

"That's good to know," I said. "So in general, succulents have magical healing properties?"

"In general, yes. They're very useful for people who are sick, and you will often find that various paranormal communities send some of their Healers here from time to time to refill their stores of succulents. Opinions on this differ based on the paranormal, but some Healers believe that the plants that grow naturally in the desert have stronger healing properties than the ones grown artificially in laboratories in each town."

"What do you think?"

"I'm not sure," Amy said with a small shrug. "I'm not a Healer, and I haven't done extensive study on the topic, so I'm afraid I can't say either way."

"Personally, I think there is something to it," Ellie said. "I can't speak for the succulents exactly, but I've definitely grown certain herbs and spices in the house, and they never seem to be quite as powerful as the ones that I get from the forest."

It was an interesting topic of conversation, but as the sun approached the horizon, the four of us realized it was time for the lesson to end, and for us to try and get the information we needed.

Right on cue, one of the golden chariots appeared. The four of us climbed into it, and a few minutes later, it dropped us off exactly where we needed to be: Caesar's Palace, the vampire bar constantly frequented by Anton.

"I really don't like it here," Amy said, looking up at the seemingly abandoned building.

"You can stay out here if you want," Ellie said. "But I think the more of us there are, the more likely we are to scare him into telling us what we want to know."

"Fine," Amy said. "But I'm only doing this because I'm sure that Professor Lei was not involved in the gambling ring at all, and I want to clear her good name since she is no longer here to do it herself."

The four of us squeezed into the entrance room and let the door close behind us before opening the second door that led into the vampire bar.

Sure enough, Anton was sitting exactly at the same table as he had been the night before. When he saw us enter, he scowled, making no effort to hide the distaste he felt in seeing us.

"What do you want this time?" he asked as we sat down across from him, letting Ellie do the talking. After all, she was way better than us at this sort of thing.

"When was the last time you spoke to Aquila?" Ellie asked.

"Why's that any of your business?"

"It's important."

"I don't care what's important to you."

"So you haven't spoken to him recently."

"I didn't say that."

This was obviously getting nowhere. Ellie obviously felt the same way, because she leaned back in the chair and crossed her arms.

"Fine. Doesn't matter anyway. The thing is, we are pretty sure we figured out who Aquila is. And Aquila is dead." As Ellie said the words, I looked carefully at Anton's face, and I might have imagined it but I thought his eyes widened a little bit for just a split second, before that same self-assured grin crept back onto his face.

"Like you would know."

"So you're not going to tell us when the last time he spoke to him was?"

"Absolutely not. I already told you more than I should have last time."

"Fine. Doesn't matter to us. Just this one over here wanted some proof," Ellie said, jerking a thumb towards Amy. "So, we figured we would ask you. Doesn't change a thing as far as we're concerned. We know who Aquila is. And he's dead. Just in case you start wondering why you can't get in touch with him."

Ellie got up from her chair and the rest of us immediately followed suit after her. As soon as we were outside, I turned towards her.

"Why did you do that? Now the conversation's ended."

Ellie grinned. "That was on purpose. Now he's been told Aquila's dead, what's the first thing he's going to do?"

"Try and find out if that's true or not," Amy said, nodding. "He's going to call her, and try and drop off some money for her, or something."

"Exactly. If the money goes, then Aquila is still alive. If it doesn't, then Aquila is dead, and his entire stream of income has dried up."

"So we are going to follow him?" I asked.

"That's right," Ellie said. "Amy, help me make everyone invisible. As soon as he comes out of that bar, we need to go after him and see where he goes."

Between Amy and Ellie both casting the spells, ten seconds later the four of us were invisible. It wasn't a moment too soon; about fifteen seconds after that Anton suddenly left via the bar's front door, looked around for a minute - probably making sure he wasn't being followed - and began walking down the street to the right.

We had him.

## CHAPTER 21

*A*s the four of us followed Anton, the only light coming from the small lamps on the side of the road, I tried to make as little noise as possible with my feet. After all, we weren't visible, but we weren't soundproof either. If Anton suspected something might be up, there was a chance that he would stop what he was doing and try to reach Aquila differently.

From time to time, he would stop and look around, and every time he did that the four of us would stop and I would hold my breath, hoping against all hope that he hadn't figured out we were here. We did stay reasonably far behind him; we were about thirty feet back at any given moment.

I had no idea where we were headed, but eventually we reached what appeared to be the main center of town. A large fountain that seemed elaborately out of place given the western theme of the rest of Desert

Plains shot water high up into the air while onlookers gasped at the sight.

To my surprise, when the water shot up from the fountain, it didn't simply come back down. Instead, it created shapes in midair: a shot of water turned into hundreds of coins, which dropped back into the fountain amid the happy cries of onlookers. The next shot turned into a horse, which galloped around the perimeter of the fountain for a moment before diving back into the water and disappearing.

"Tina come on," Sara said to me, feeling around until she grabbed my hand. "He's over there."

I was a little bit surprised that Anton would dare leave things for Aquila in such an open environment. After all, this seemed to be the center of Desert Plains. I had expected their hand-off to take place somewhere empty, where no one would see them. But at the same time, I supposed in a way this made sense. It was easy to hide in a crowd, after all.

Sara pulled me away until we reached a quiet corner underneath the entrance to a souvenir shop that was closed for the night.

"Can you see him?" Ellie asked.

"I do," Amy said. "He's by one of the corners of the fountain. I suspect that's their drop-off point."

"Whatever they drop-off, couldn't anyone find it?" I asked.

"No," Amy said. "In all likelihood, they're using magic to hide the money. It's possible to cast a spell on something so that only the intended receiver can see it."

"So it doesn't matter if they do their hand-off in the middle of the busiest part of town," Ellie nodded.

"Exactly. It makes it much more difficult for law enforcement to find them, since it's not like they're hiding somewhere handing things off in secret. They're doing it right out in the open."

"Surely, Aquila is using the same spell as we are, though," Sara said. "There is no way whoever it is - whether we are right about Aquila being Professor Lei, or if it's someone else - is coming out into the open to collect anything."

"Agreed," Ellie said. "So if we can't see Aquila, and we can't keep an eye on the package because it's been magically enchanted, how are we going to be able to tell if Aquila even came?"

"I think there's a spell," Amy said, squeezing her eyes shut. "It's not a Jupiter spell. But I read about it not long ago. It comes from the coven of Saturn, which is an air coven. The spell essentially covers an area and negates any spells cast in that area."

"So we would be able to see not only Aquila, but also the bag?" I asked.

Amy nodded. "Yes. And not only that, but Aquila would be unaware that we have cast the spell. Only the person who cast the spell can see any difference. So to Aquila, everything would look normal."

"Great," Ellie said. "Let's do it, quickly, before Aquila comes and we miss our chance."

Amy nodded. "Everyone, link arms. I'm going to cast this spell, and if we link together, the magic will affect us all and so you will also be able to see Aquila when he or she comes."

I couldn't help but notice Amy's use of the word 'when'. She was obviously still 100% convinced that Professor Lei was not Aquila. I was ready to see if she was right. The four of us spent a few minutes trying to hook arms; it was a little bit difficult given as we were all still invisible, but eventually we were all hooked up.

"All right, everyone focus your energy towards me," Amy said. I didn't really know what Amy meant by that, and I didn't want to waste any time by asking, so I simply cleared my head as best as I could and felt the energy build up inside of me. To my surprise, the energy inside of me felt like it wanted to escape through the arm I was linked to. This must've been exactly what Amy wanted. I relaxed my body and let the energy go, feeling it rush away from me and towards Amy.

"*Saturn, ruler of time, hail! Whatever spells there be, uncover the veil!*"

I wasn't sure if anything was supposed to happen, but a thin, white mist began flowing from Amy's wand and towards the crowd. Eventually, the mist covered the entire main square, but no one else seemed to notice anything.

"Did it work?" Ellie asked.

"I think so," Amy said. "Everything underneath the white mist should have its magic revealed to us."

"There," Sara said. "By the edge of the fountain, a couple of people just moved and I got a look at a black bag that wasn't there a minute ago."

"Excellent," I said, a grin crossing my features. "That means the spell worked. Now, all we need to do is wait for someone to show up - or, more likely, not show up to pick up that bag."

"Just you wait," Amy said. "I guarantee you someone will be here. Professor Lei was not Aquila."

Two minutes later, Amy was proved right.

I let out a gasp and pointed, even though none of the others could see what I was pointing at, as Alex, the professor I had met in the coven chapel, strode through the crowd and grabbed the bag off the ground.

## CHAPTER 22

"*N*o way," Ellie said quietly, noticing the same thing that I had.

"Not Professor Lei," Amy whispered, the betrayal in her voice evident.

"Well, you were right, Amy," Sara said. "Professor Lei wasn't Aquila."

"I can't believe it," Amy said.

"Well, what are we going to do?" I asked. "Believe it or not, I think we know who Aquila is now."

"We need to follow her," Ellie said. "But first, we're going visible again. This is going to be way too hard to manage if we don't know where we all are."

Ellie and Amy quickly cast the spell making us all visible once more, and when we turned to look, Alex Lyn was just leaving with the bag of money.

"Let's go," I said, rushing towards where she was. I had no idea what we were going to do, but I knew we had to do something. After all, if nothing else, Alex Lyn was almost certainly responsible for Chief Enforcer King's disappearance. We had to stop her.

The four of us began moving towards her, passing through the throngs of people. On the bright side, there were so many people around that we just melded into the crowd and didn't stand out at all. On the other hand, it made it harder to keep an eye on Alexandra as she moved away from the fountain.

I could see the edge of the white mist not far from where she was; if she passed through it, Amy's spell would no longer be functional, and she would be invisible once more.

"Professor Lyn!" Amy called out. It was a good idea; Amy was the one of us who probably knew Alex the best, given all the time she spent in the Academy.

Alex paused for a second, then looked down at herself before looking around carefully. I could imagine her confusion; she must have expected that being invisible, no one would know she was there.

"Professor Lyn, it's me, Amy!" Amy called out once more, and she must have realized something was wrong and she was visible after all, because Alex stopped and put on a polite smile, hoisting the bag over her shoulder like it was nothing.

"Ah, Amy. What a lovely surprise. I wasn't expecting to see you here at all."

The four of us caught up to her, and Alex looked at us all with a small smile on her face. I imagined she couldn't figure out at all how we had caught up to her.

"What have you got there, Professor?" Ellie asked, motioning to the shoulder bag.

"This? Oh, nothing. Just some stuff I need to take back to Western Woods."

"Are you sure that's all it is? Listen, we were here looking for Chief Enforcer King, and we were wondering if you knew anything about it," Sara said.

"Chief Enforcer King? Why would I know anything about that?"

"Well, you know, what with you being Aquila and all and Chief Enforcer King working to break up your little gang of gamblers, we figured the two might very well be linked," Ellie said.

Okay. So we were definitely going with the 'tell her straight away what we knew' method. That was fine. After all, we were in the middle of the busiest square in Desert Plains. There was a limit to what Alex could do to us here.

She narrowed her eyes at us. "I'm afraid I don't have a clue what you're talking about."

"Right. That bag on your shoulder totally isn't filled with money, and it totally didn't get dropped off here by Anton the vampire."

Alex looked over at Amy, imagining that she would be the most likely to be on her side. "You can't honestly believe any of this," she said, but Amy simply crossed her arms.

"How could you do something like this? You're a professor at the Academy, doesn't that mean anything to you?"

"That's why I did it," Alex said suddenly. Apparently, realizing that even Amy didn't believe her was the last straw, and she was willing to admit to everything. "I've spent my entire life teaching the next generation of witches and wizards everything they know. Do you know what state the coven would be in if it wasn't for me and the other professors? We would be in shambles, because no one would know how to use magic. We are the most important people in the coven, because we teach the next generation to use magic, and to use it well. And yet, they pay us a pittance. Sure, it's enough to live on, but shouldn't somebody in a position as important as mine make more money? So, I started coming to Desert Plains for fun. But I quickly realized there was a market here. It was prime for the taking. Sure, there was plenty of spells and magic to prevent cheating, but since when has math been cheating? You can't test for it, because it's an ability somebody has in their brain."

Suddenly, things began to make sense. "So when Chief Enforcer King realized that Aquila had to be somebody from Western Woods, she asked Professor Lei for help," I said. I was shooting in the dark, but I had a sneaking suspicion I was on the right track.

"That's right," Alex said. "It was too bad, too. Chief Enforcer King had been trying for ages to find out who

I was, but she never got anywhere close to figuring it out. She must have realized somehow that Aquila was simply using advanced math to win all of that money, and brought in Professor Lei to help her figure out who."

"You were in coven headquarters the day Professor Lei was killed," I said, my mind going back to the list of people in coven headquarters that Amy had brought home.

"I was," Alex said. "I didn't have any classes to teach that day, so I went in on the guise of preparing for the next day. But Mai wasn't being very talkative. I realized she had figured out who I was. She had to. The two of us shared classes from time to time, and if anyone knew how my mathematical brain worked, it was her. And if anyone else in the coven had the mathematical skills to figure out what was going on, it was also her. So I had to get rid of her."

I let out a sigh. The murderer had nothing to do with Mai Lei cheating on her husband, or with Kelly and her problem. It was all greed with Alex trying to hide her criminal activities for a little while longer.

"You had to know that killing Professor Lei wasn't going to be a permanent solution," I said. "You had to get rid of Chief Enforcer King, too. What did you do? You made Kelly do it, didn't you?"

Alex laughed, a cold laugh with not a trace of humor in it. "That idiot. She thought I would let her get away with owing me thousands of Abras? Of course not. I didn't make her kill Professor Lei; I figured she was too much of an idiot to handle that without getting caught, and I imagined if she did get caught she would flip on me immediately. Instead, I had her call Chief Enforcer King to lure her into a trap."

"Have you killed the Chief Enforcer?" Amy asked.

"No. It would look too suspicious. I'm brewing a potion, instead."

Ellie gasped. "A forgetfulness potion? That's incredibly cruel."

"It's what needs to happen. I realized I couldn't kill both Mai and Chief Enforcer King without the two of them being linked, but I can make Chief Enforcer King disappear until the potion is ready."

"It takes a full month for a forgetfulness potion to be created," Ellie said.

"That's right," Alex replied. "In a month, Chief Enforcer King will wake up in a town far away from here, with no memory of anything. Eventually, she will be taken back to Western Woods when they find out where she's from, and everyone will assume that she had her mind wiped in the course of doing her duties."

"What about us?" I asked. "We know everything now."

Alex laughed again. "No one knows I'm here. No one knows I ever come to Desert Plains. When your bodies show up, there will be no suspects. Maybe Anton. But who cares, he's just a stupid vampire."

"Right. Like you're going to kill us in the middle of this crowd," Ellie said, crossing her arms.

"You think I haven't realized that you're the only ones who can see me?" Alex asked. "I don't know what kind of magic you did, but no one's ever going to know that it was me."

She lifted her wand just as Ellie shouted, "Run!"

## CHAPTER 23

*I* didn't need to be told twice. As soon as Ellie shouted to run, I did exactly what my instincts told me to: I ran headlong into the fountain. After all, the one thing we did know was that I came from a water coven, and I was inherently more comfortable in the water than anywhere else.

Just as I splashed into the water, I heard a roar and a flash of light passed before my eyes a split second before I closed them, holding my breath as the water enveloped me. I could only hope that my friends had gotten away from whatever Alex did as well.

I came back up for air a moment later, and the scene that greeted me was one of complete chaos. Everywhere around me, people were running. Everyone who had been in the square was running for cover and a giant hole in the ground told me exactly why: someone had been attacked.

My eyes scanned quickly, trying to find my friends. Sara was running with the crowd; I could see her trying to get away without being seen. Ellie was lying slumped against one of the wooden buildings. My heart dropped, but a moment later, I saw her hand twitch. She was hurt, but she wasn't dead. Thank goodness.

As the crowd moved away, two forms near the crater in the ground stood out. One was Alex, her wand pointed directly in front of her. The other, in the same position, was Amy. They stood facing one another; the tips of Amy's hair was burned, but she stood strong.

"You killed one of my favorite professors," Amy said through gritted teeth. "I'm not going to let you get away with this."

"Please. You've always thought you were a way better witch than everybody else, but the reality is you're just a little bit above average. How could you possibly think you could defeat me?"

"Like this," Amy said, waving her wand towards the professor. I suddenly realized that Amy's ability to cast spells without saying the words was incredibly handy; Alex had absolutely no way of knowing what spell Amy was using until it was on her.

I jumped out of the fountain and began moving towards Ellie, trying subtly to sneak past the battleground where Amy had just shot a bolt of thunder towards Alex. Alex, however, had managed to put up a shield blocking the thunderbolt from hitting her and was attacking back.

I had to trust that Amy could hold her own; Ellie was the one who needed help right now.

Making my way towards her, my eyes widened as I saw a deep pool of blood forming beneath her. Looking closely, a large gash on her arm was the source. What on earth was I going to do?

I didn't know any spells that could help. I didn't even know if there *were* any spells that could help with this. What I did know was that Ellie was losing blood, and fast. If something didn't happen soon, she was going to die right here.

Looking over at Alex and Amy, who were still deep in their fight, I suddenly remembered what Amy had taught me only a couple of hours earlier.

I needed to get to the desert.

Silently apologizing to Amy for not helping take on Alex - though it wasn't like I was going to be a great help anyway - I rushed away from the scene and looked around wildly. Where on earth was the desert? I needed to get out of town and find an elgans blue plant.

One of those golden chariots popped up in front of me right then and there, and I climbed in like my life depended on it. Technically, it was Ellie's life that depended on it.

"Go, go," I shouted at the chariot, and it darted off, faster than normal. "As fast as you can!"

The chariot darted through the streets of Desert Plains so quickly I was starting to feel a little bit carsick, but that didn't matter. Less than two minutes later we were out of town and the chariot screeched to a stop, sending me flying over to the other side and into the far wall. Gathering myself up off the floor, I practically leapt out of the chariot, yelling at it to stay there. I didn't have time to wait for another chariot to arrive.

The magical chariots that took you exactly where you needed to be were perfect. I found myself standing directly in front of an elgans blue plant. Ripping the whole thing out of the ground, I leapt back into the chariot and slammed the door close behind me.

"Again! As fast as you can! Get me back to Ellie!"

By the time I jumped out of the chariot once more and rushed towards my friend, the pool of blood underneath her had gotten bigger. I ripped off one of the leaves from the plant and began chewing it like crazy, and when it had turned into a giant pile of mush I spat the whole thing back out into my palm and pressed it against the large gash on Ellie's arm.

I really, really hoped that I had remembered my lesson properly.

For the first couple of seconds, Ellie's blood seeped between my fingers as I pressed the elgans blue mush against her arm. But then, the flow began to ebb, and a moment later the bleeding stopped completely.

I was so relieved tears began running down my face.

Mashing up another leaf in my mouth, just in case, I pressed this new mash against Ellie's arm as well, and with my other hand I checked for a pulse. It was faint, but it was still there. Ellie was still alive.

"Is she okay?" I suddenly heard Sara's voice ask quietly, and I looked over to see her coming towards us. "I ran away, but I had to come back. I didn't want to get involved in the fight; I figured I would only be a liability."

"Same," I said. "This plant is saving Ellie. I think this is all I can do."

The two of us looked over at the fighters - student and professor - and it was obvious that the student was winning. Alex was panting, covered in dirt, and it looked like even the act of pointing her wand towards Amy was taking a toll on her. On the other hand, Amy looked completely poised, cool and collected. She pointed her wand at Alex and spoke.

"We can finish this right now. If you're willing to hand yourself in, and tell everyone what happened to Chief Enforcer King, I'm sure a deal can be worked out for leniency."

"Leniency? What's the point? No one's going to be lenient to a witch who killed a member of her own coven. Besides, if I'm going down, then Chief Enforcer King is going down forever as well."

Before I knew what had happened, Alex pointed her

wand at the fountain, then ran directly into it. As soon as she touched the water she began to scream, a horrible sound that filled the night air. She disappeared into the water, her cries eventually cut off, and Amy rushed to the edge. She touched the water with a single finger, then pulled it back, shaking it.

"She turned the fountain into acid," Amy called out as she ran towards us. "I guess Alex would rather have died then gone to prison. Is Ellie okay?"

"I think she will be," I said. "We need to get her to a Healer, though."

Right on cue, one of the golden chariots appeared, and the three of us managed to lift Ellie up and get her in before closing the door and speeding off towards the Desert Plains hospital.

"Is that elgens blue?" Amy asked, nodding towards the mush that my hand was still holding on the wound. "I knew all of those lessons would come in handy."

## CHAPTER 24

*A* couple of hours later, Ellie woke up, after emergency help from the Healers, who commended my quick thinking and using the succulent's powers to save her life.

"If you hadn't done it when you did, she wouldn't have made it," one of the Healers told me. "You should be very proud of yourself."

I only nodded in response; it had been a very stressful day. We had solved Professor Lei's murder, and Alex was dead, but we still didn't know where Chief Enforcer King was. And the only person who could help us had committed suicide, probably in part to stop us from ever being able to find her.

As soon as Ellie woke up she wanted to know what happened, and we all recounted the story.

"I knew you were better than half those professors at the Academy," Ellie told Amy, and while Amy waved away the compliment, I couldn't help but notice a small blush of happiness crawl up her cheeks.

"So where's Chief Enforcer King?" Ellie asked.

"We don't know," Amy said.

"Well, that's exactly what we're doing now," Ellie said, getting out of bed. "She's been missing for days already, we're not going to let her wither away and die in whatever hole Professor Lyn has been keeping her in."

"Have you asked the Healers if it's okay for you to go?" Amy asked.

"I'm awake, aren't I? That's good enough."

Amy definitely didn't agree that it was good enough, but after asking a Healer if Ellie could leave, the Healer said it was fine. The five of us immediately made our way back to Western Woods, where we were absolutely going to find Chief Enforcer King.

Sara volunteered to find Lita and tell her what had happened while Ellie, Amy, and I did our best to find where Chief Enforcer King had been hidden.

"Should we try her house?" Ellie suggested as soon as we got into town. "Maybe she's keeping her there?"

Amy nodded. "Okay. But I don't know where Professor Lyn lived. Check her office first so we can find an address?"

"Done," Ellie replied. "Although, to be honest, I'm surprised you don't have home addresses for every single person who's ever taught you. How else can you stalk them to try and get a better mark when they only give you 90% on tests?"

Amy stuck her tongue out at Ellie. "I'll let you know I haven't gotten below 95% on a test in over seven years."

Ellie burst out laughing as we made our way into coven headquarters, rushing past Estelle Thurman who was watching the door and making our way upstairs to the Professors' offices and classrooms.

I followed Ellie and Amy, who, unlike me, knew where they were going, and entered into a sparsely-decorated classroom whose walls were covered in mathematical posters and charts.

"If we find anything that might indicate a secret hideout or something like that, we need to check it out," Amy said.

"How about using that spell you used in Desert Plains?" I asked. "After all, that one revealed any magic that we couldn't see. It should work here too, right?"

"Good idea," Amy nodded. She closed her eyes, pulled out her wand, and re-cast the spell. Once again, white mist began to flow from Amy's wand, and she walked around the room, pointing the wand every-where until finally the entire room was enveloped in the fine mist. There was nothing.

"Okay," Ellie said. "Now we look for anything with her home address on it."

Before we got a chance to, however, Kelly Treach entered the room. She stopped as soon as she saw the mist, waving some of it away from her face with her hand.

"Is it true that Professor Lyn killed herself?"

"Yes," I said to her. "We know that she was the one who made you lure Chief Enforcer King into a trap."

"She did," Kelly said. "I felt so awful about it. But I didn't feel like I had any other choice. I thought Chief Enforcer King was dead, but Sara says she isn't?"

"That's right," I replied. "Alexa told us she's keeping Chief Enforcer King alive, but that she was working on a potion to erase her memory."

"I can help you," Kelly said. "I didn't say anything before, because I thought Chief Enforcer King was dead. But I'm pretty sure I know where she is."

~

Fifteen minutes later, the three of us were walking through the woods.

"Are you sure she was out here?" Amy asked, and Kelly nodded.

"Yes. I'm sure. As soon as Anton told me that Aquila wanted me to get Chief Enforcer King to come to the outskirts of the woods, I knew someone from town had to be involved. After all, why else go after Chief Enforcer King? So I cast a tracking spell on Chief Enforcer King, which was never detected."

"Smart," Amy nodded.

"Maybe the first smart thing I've ever done," Kelly

said glumly. "I've made so many mistakes, if it turns out Chief Enforcer King is dead, I'll never forgive myself."

"Well, you're doing what you can now to make amends for your mistakes," I said reassuringly. "That has to count for something, right?"

After about five hundred feet of following the path, Kelly motioned to the right. "She's down there, about two hundred more feet along.

Ellie, Amy, Kelly, and I pushed through the brush, when finally we reached a small clearing with some rocks at the far end. "There," Kelly said, pointing to the rocks. "That's where my tracker says she is."

Amy waved her wand at the rock at the front of the entrance, but nothing happened. She frowned. "Professor Lyn must have cast a spell here."

"Definitely," Ellie said. "Otherwise, the shifters would have been able to follow the smell and find Chief Enforcer King no problem."

"Of course," Amy said. "Give me a few minutes, and I'll have all of the spells canceled."

Sure enough, a couple of minutes later Amy waved her wand at the rock again, and this time it dislodged, showing a small hole in which Chief Enforcer King was lying.

"Chief Enforcer!" I called out, running towards her. As soon as I reached the blonde lion shifter, I feared the worst. Her eyes were closed, and she didn't look like she was alive. But, putting two fingers to her neck, I felt a pulse. "She's alive," I called out to the others, who all rushed over.

"We need to get her to a Healer," Amy said. "She's obviously under a spell, and I don't want to wake her from it without knowing what it is."

I immediately texted Sara our location, telling her to come with a broom.

"Sara's on her way," I said. Five minutes later, she arrived, and without a single word loaded up Chief Enforcer King in front of her on the broom.

"I'll get her to the hospital as fast as I can," Sara said.

As soon as Sara left, Kelly broke down in tears. "I thought I had killed her. I thought Professor Lyn had killed Chief Enforcer King, and that it was all because of me."

Ellie put a comforting hand on Kelly's shoulder. "She's alive. Thanks to you. If you hadn't put that tracking spell on Chief Enforcer King, I don't think we ever would have found her."

I had to agree with Ellie. Kelly had done something wrong, but at the same time, she had done what she could to rectify her mistake. I really hoped whoever was in charge of sorting these things out would be lenient with her.

# EPILOGUE

"*O*kay, are you ready?" Sara asked, and I gave her the thumbs up. We were recording her video to apply for the new broom flying competition being run by the same people who did the duels. I had my phone out, video set to record, in the middle of the coven gardens as Sara flew up onto her broom and up into the sky faster than a speeding bullet.

I squinted as she flew into the sun, then drove down at top speed, pulling up just in time to miss the ground, blades of grass swaying from the wind of her broom as she swept past.

Sara darted in and out between some trees, showing her agility and skill on the broom with a deftness I knew she had but that still surprised me every time I saw it.

Watching Sara on a broom was like watching a ballet dancer. She had an elegance that anyone would envy, but at the same time a strength unmatched by anyone else that I knew.

There was absolutely no way she would not get chosen for this new sport.

I had a long conversation with Sara about it after everything calmed down a little bit once Chief Enforcer King was found.

The Chief Enforcer was fine. After Sara took her to the hospital, the Healers did their thing and figured out which spell was used to put her under, and managed to reverse it. Chief Enforcer King woke up, and found out exactly what had happened to her, and to Professor Lei.

Chief Enforcer King explained that Professor Lei had figured out that Aquila was actually Alex Lyn, and that they had planned on arresting her that day. She didn't remember anything after that.

After being told of Kelly's role in leading her to the trap, but also discovering that Kelly was instrumental in finding Chief Enforcer King once more, Chief Enforcer King decided to be lenient with Kelly, and instead of going to prison, Kelly would be working for the community, unpaid, for the next year.

Kelly sobbed with gratitude when Chief Enforcer King told her that was her sentence. She swore she would get help for the gambling, and promised to do everything she could to make up for the pain she had caused.

The following morning, Sara and I found ourselves

alone in the house, and I brought up the topic of the broom flying competition.

"I get the impression that you don't really want to do it," I said to Sara. "Am I wrong? I just want you to know, if you're not interested, then I will fully support you in that decision."

Sara sighed. "You're not imagining it, but it isn't that I'm not interested. Honestly, nothing sounds more amazing to me, and I would love to do it. But the thing is, there is no guarantee. Broom flying is the only thing I have in my life that I'm good at. It's the most important thing to me, and what if they don't take me? What happens then?"

I considered Sara's words for a minute. I could definitely see where she was coming from. She really wanted to do this, but she was scared. "Then what happens is you're still the best witch on a broom from Western Woods, but you're not going to spend the rest of your life wondering what might have happened. What will you regret more: trying, failing, but knowing that you gave it your best, or never trying at all?"

Sara mulled over my words. I decided to keep going, since after all, I felt like I was on a bit of a roll. "You don't even need to tell anyone you tried out. Let's go out now, take an audition video, and then I'll send it to you. You don't even need to tell me if you submit it."

"Okay," Sara said finally, making up her mind and jumping up from the couch. "Let's go do this."

That was how I found myself now taking a cell

phone video of Sara as she displayed all of her skills on a broom, leaving me completely awestruck. There was absolutely no way she wasn't going to get selected for this. There just couldn't be. She was too good.

After she finished flying around, including a dip into the water where she flew straight down into the lake in the middle before coming right back up and shooting straight up into the sky like some sort of bird of prey, Sara landed directly in front of me and shot a grin to the camera.

"My name is Sara Neach, and I'm going to be crowned the best broom rider in the paranormal world."

I turned off the video and grinned at my friend. I had no idea if what she said was true. I didn't even know if she was going to send in the audition tape. But I did know I was so thankful to have a friend like her, and all the others as well. No matter what, Sara was a winner in my book.

# ALSO BY SAMANTHA SILVER

First of all, I wanted to thank you for reading this book. I well and truly hope you enjoyed reading this book as much as I loved writing it.

If you enjoyed Three's a Coven I'd really appreciate it if you could take a moment and leave a review for the book on Amazon, to help other readers find the book as well.

Want to read more of Tina's adventures? The fourth book in the Western Woods Mystery series, Four Leaf Clovers, will be released in January 2019,

## Other Western Woods Mysteries

Back to Spell One (Western Woods Mystery #1)

Two Peas in a Potion (Western Woods Mystery #2)

Four Leaf Clovers (Western Woods Mystery #4)

## Willow Bay Witches Mysteries

The Purr-fect Crime (Willow Bay Witches #1)

Barking up the Wrong Tree (Willow Bay Witches #2)

Just Horsing Around (Willow Bay Witches #3)

Lipstick on a Pig (Willow Bay Witches #4)

A Grizzly Discovery (Willow Bay Witches #5)

Sleeping with the Fishes (Willow Bay Witches #6)

Get your Ducks in a Row (Willow Bay Witches #7)

Busy as a Beaver (Willow Bay Witches #8)

## Magical Bookshop Mysteries

Alice in Murderland (Magical Bookshop Mystery #1)

Murder on the Oregon Express (Magical Bookshop Mystery #2)

The Very Killer Caterpillar (Magical Bookshop Mystery #3)

Death Quixote (Magical Bookshop Mystery #4)

Pride and Premeditation (Magical Bookshop Mystery #5)

## Moonlight Cove Mysteries

Witching Aint's Easy (Moonlight Cove Mystery #1)

Witching for the Best (Moonlight Cove Mystery #2)

Thank your Lucky Spells (Moonlight Cove Mystery #3)

A Perfect Spell (Moonlight Cove Mystery #4)

## California Witching Mysteries

Witches and Wine (California Witching Mystery #1)

Poison and Pinot (California Witching Mystery #2)

Merlot and Murder (California Witching Mystery #3)

## Cassie Coburn Mysteries

Poison in Paddington (Cassie Coburn Mystery #1)

Bombing in Belgravia (Cassie Coburn Mystery #2)

Whacked in Whitechapel (Cassie Coburn Mystery #3)

Strangled in Soho (Cassie Coburn Mystery #4)

Stabbed in Shoreditch (Cassie Coburn Mystery #5)

Killed in King's Cross (Cassie Coburn Mystery #6)

## Ruby Bay Mysteries

Death Down Under (Ruby Bay Mystery #1)

Arson in Australia (Ruby Bay Mystery #2)

The Killer Kangaroo (Ruby Bay Mystery #3)

Samantha Silver lives in British Columbia, Canada, along with her husband and a little old doggie named Terra. She loves animals, skiing and of course, writing cozy mysteries.

You can connect with Samantha online on Facebook.

Printed in Great Britain
by Amazon